Act of Will

an Andersson Dexter novel

M. Darusha Wehm

Books by M. Darusha Wehm

Beautiful Red
Children of Arkadia

Andersson Dexter novels

Self Made
Act of Will
The Beauty of Our Weapons

More information at http://darusha.ca

Act of Will

By M. Darusha Wehm

Published by *in potentia press*

Copyright 2011 M. Darusha Wehm

ISBN 978-0-9737467-5-4

http://darusha.ca/actofwill

I'm guided by a signal in the heavens.
I'm guided by this birthmark on my skin.
I'm guided by the beauty of our weapons.

- *First We Take Manhattan*, Leonard Cohen

CHAPTER ONE

LUIS HARKER WAS not a particularly emotional man, but he was crying now. Big, racking sobs convulsed his body, straining his bound hands against the back of the chair he was tied to, the cuffs digging into his wrists. When the man had first put the restraints on him, Luis found himself, lucid through the fear for a brief moment, wondering if they were the new electromagnetic cuffs that all the Security guys were talking about at work. It had been a long time since he had been able to think about anything like that.

He barely even noticed the room he was in, on the face of it a tiny anonymous box, like every other apartment he had seen. But a closer look showed the room for what it was missing — there was no storage area, no zapper for heating food. Just a stained mattress, a door that Luis might have guessed led to the lav had he been able to think about it. And the chair. All of Luis' attention was riveted to the chair in the middle of the room.

It was a typical metal chair, the kind you would find in the waiting room of an upgrade salon or a cheap food booth. There was nothing remarkable about it, other than the fact that Luis had been tied to it for what felt like an eternity, bound by thick polymer rope that seemed to get tighter the more he struggled. He had stopped struggling a long time ago; now the uncontrollable movement of his body as he sobbed was the only tension against his restraints.

• • •

When the man had first grabbed him, Luis had put up a fight. He had been leaving work, the sky already dark but the lights of the city bright enough that he felt he should have seen the man crouching in the small alleyway. But while Luis was walking to the train stop, he was going online after a long day at work, checking his messages and scanning the news boards. He had made that walk 260 days a year for three years and he barely even watched where he was going any more. With his display overlaid on his vision, he could see just enough to avoid the other commuters while he surfed the boards and answered mail, but that had always been enough before.

Luis was in the middle of reading an article about a new brand of food bars which promised increased mental acuity and focus as well as the usual nutritional supplements, when he felt the wind go out of him. He was dazed, but he could still see through the words and images on his display and he saw a figure duck in front of him and take what looked like a small metal box from a pocket. Luis had no idea what was happening, but instinct told him it was not a good thing, so he tried to knock the box from the other person's hand.

Even though he worked in the physical upgrade industry and wore the body of a fashionable young man about town, Luis had never been all that interested in physical things. Like many people, he lived his recreational life online, in the virtual world Marionette City which he accessed through his neural implants. So, he was completely unprepared for the pain and loss of balance that came when his hand made contact with the metal box and in the moment of his confusion, the other person found an opening. The box swung up and Luis felt rather than saw an arc of electricity shoot from the box toward his face. Everything slowly faded to gray and Luis felt himself fall to the ground. He felt hands holding his wrists together and binding them with the lightweight restraints that his addled mind incongruously focussed on. Then he was out.

• • •

When he opened his eyes, he was in the room, tied to the chair with his wrists behind his back. He was alone. Of course, he screamed for help, tried to go online and call for help, but his screams went unanswered and he found his connection to everywherenet scrambled. The small, still lucid part of his brain guessed that whatever hit him from the metal box had screwed with his implants, but he kept trying to connect, over and over again until the full implication of his situation caught up with him and he began to cry uncontrollably. He was going to die, after that crazy fucker did god only knows what to him first. Luis threw up all over himself.

He waited, alone and afraid, smelling the stink of his vomit and sweat. With every minute that passed, he became more afraid, less able to think clearly. By the time the apartment door opened, Luis couldn't even speak. He simply thrashed at his bounds as the man entered, grunting incoherently as the man slowly walked toward him, Luis' eyes wild with pure animal terror. Even though he was looking right at the man, there was no way Luis would ever have been able to identify him, even if he lived. He never even noticed the knife.

• • •

It gleamed as if it were a brand new laser edged cutter, but it was old. The short handle was made of fossilized bone, worn smooth and shiny by the sweat of untold numbers of hands. The blade, Damascus steel, was inlaid with an intricate pattern — wavy like water — as it had been folded and forged by hand. The steel was honed to a razor edge, its tip a dagger's pinpoint. It was beautiful.

The hand which held the knife, loose and comfortable, belonged to a man who was as ordinary as the weapon was remarkable. He had a body sculpted by the nutrients and chemicals in budget food bars — young, thin, muscular, healthy and utterly nondescript. His face was dotted with the small metal studs most everyone wore, implants which upgraded the neural interface with everywherenet. He could have been anyone; Luis could easily have been his brother. Even his voice was unremarkable, but Luis jumped when the man spoke.

"I'm sorry about this," the man said softly, tracing the polymer bounds with the tip of the knife. "I don't usually keep people like this for so long, but I was unavoidably detained. I'm sorry; it must be very uncomfortable."

Luis struggled to make sense of the man's words, tried to formulate something to say, something to get him out of this. "Please," he croaked, his voice hoarse from shouting, "please. Let me go."

The man laughed, the sound surprisingly light. There was no trace of cruelty in his voice when he said, "I'm sorry, but I can't do that." He drew the knife absently across Luis' arm, a thin line of blood welling up in its wake. "Make no mistake," he said, "I am going to kill you. But there's no reason why we can't both enjoy it." He pulled the small metal box from a pocket and Luis felt the spark of lightning again. One of the nodes in his face burned for a fraction of a second, then he felt the sensation change to one of intense pleasure.

The man began the work with the knife and Luis felt physical ecstasy like he never had imagined. He spent twenty glorious minutes before he finally died.

CHAPTER TWO

ANDERSSON DEXTER WAS having a bad day and it wasn't even noon yet. Things had started out well enough — his room had brightened for him just the way he liked, waking him easily out of a deep sleep. He didn't even have a twinge of a hangover. But then he opened his eyes and saw the walls of his small room and he remembered that he wasn't in Europa any more. He was back in the city, alone and Annabelle was thousands of klicks away again.

He had been back for nearly two weeks and every morning was like this, though some days were better than other. This one was worse. When he got to work he was already in a sour mood. He sat at his desk and logged into the office's network a couple of minutes early. Right on the dot of nine, a little light flashed at the corner of his vision and a customer's details began scrolling before his eyes. A chime sounded and Dex could hear the faint hum of an open voice line. "Barrett and Brar Upgrades," he said, faux-cheerfully, "How may I help you make a better you?"

Dex had put in a decade at B&B and he'd been working as a CSR for a long time before he got that job. He'd been threatened, sworn at, bullied, despised and mocked more times than he could count and like anyone in that business, it rarely gave him a moment's pause. But he was cranky and the last thing he needed to hear first thing in the morning was the stream of invective this customer unleashed. It was twenty minutes before he got the woman to calm down and an hour before he finally resolved the call. A good long time over the twelve minutes that headquarters expected each call should average and another black mark next to the name Andersson Dexter.

Dex grabbed a food brick from his desk drawer and tore it open. He took a large bite of the glutinous cube and slowly chewed while he typed up the notes from his call with Miss-Not-Ms. Mary Stiles, nemesis customer of the day. While he typed, he activated his covert program that allowed him to have access to the everywherenet from inside the B&B system. The firms kept their systems locked down, ostensibly for security reasons, but mostly to keep employees for wasting company time on other activities. Like Dex was about to do now.

While finishing his tasks for B&B, Dex logged into another system, this one for an organization with no official name, but which he and his cohorts called The Cubicle Men. When he wasn't enduring calls from customers like Mary Stiles, Dex was a detective, solving cases for people who had no legitimate place to turn. The only law enforcement was the private Security arms of the firms and they only cared about problems that affected them. If you had no job, or only a low level one, there was nowhere to fight for you if you were cheated or stolen from. And if your problem was in an area that the firms disapproved of, then you had no chance. Except with people like Dex, who were employed at places like B&B but, unbeknown to their employers, were really on the clock for the Cubicle Men.

There was no new case for him, though, which soured his mood even more. He sighed aloud and his new office neighbour, a mousy looking man whose name Dex had never bothered to learn, sharply looked up. Dex scowled at the man, who quickly ducked his head down again. Dex checked the clock just barely visible in the corner of his vision. It was only ten minutes past eleven.

• • •

After his shift at B&B, Dex rode the train home. Before he even reached the sidewalk in front of Barrett and Brar's fifty-storey building, he was logged into M City, headed for Three Card Monte's bar. Monte's was in a seedy part of Marionette City, the virtual world that was becoming more and more the social hub for most people. Dex liked the virtual neighbourhood; it was dark, a little gloomy and nothing like the rest of Marionette City, with its bright, shiny animations and impossible designs.

Annabelle Lewis was waiting for him when his avatar walked into the bar. Unlike many people, Dex chose his avatar to look pretty similar to that way he looked in the physical world. He didn't own an antique charcoal three piece suit like the one he wore in M City and he didn't think you could even buy hats like the one his avatar always had pulled low over his eyes, but otherwise it was just him. Annabelle noticed him arrive and waved from a table in a dark corner of the bar.

Dex knew that her avatar was a pretty faithful representation of her real physical body, too, but he also knew that it hadn't always been that way. She had visited Dex previously, but on his first trip to see her he'd had quite a surprise when he arrived. He discovered that she had, as she put it, simply had her physical body adjusted to conform to the image she had of herself. Dex wondered if it was really just a coincidence that she'd finally decided to get the work done just before he visited for the first time, but it had never come up in the week he spent in her spacious flat in Nice. He wasn't sure he ever wanted to have that conversation.

He had to admit that Annabelle was beautiful. She had the same slim body that most people wore, thanks to the powerful engineering in the ubiquitous food bricks and tonics everyone but the very rich and very poor lived off. Dex was impressed with the work she'd had done, but it was her eyes that really drew Dex in to her and they hadn't changed at all. He wondered how much she had paid some designer for her avatar, since even in M City they danced with the same sense of humour and joie de vivre he saw in the baby blues she wore on the streets. Dex approached the table and found that his day turned around at the sight of Annabelle. He couldn't help smiling, both with his body and his avatar. He half-watched half-felt himself embrace Annabelle and felt a frisson of revulsion at the strangeness of the virtual experience.

He hoped that his reaction hadn't been translated into his hug by the complex programming that controlled avatars in the virtual world and reminded himself that he had been getting much better at ignoring those feelings. He pulled back and smiled at Annabelle, who grinned at him. "Nice hat," she said, her eyes dropping to the dark felt in Dex's right hand.

"It's the same one as always, kiddo," Dex said.

"I know," Annabelle answered, sitting back down. "It's still nice."

Dex sat across from her and ordered his usual — a no-stimulant rum and ginger beer — from the pretend human bartender program. Annabelle was sipping what looked like a gin fizz and Dex figured was probably a complex cocktail of neural stimulants that she used like Dex used real rum. As if reading his mind, she lifted her drink to gesture at his and asked, "So, you have a wet dark and stormy going at home?"

Dex smiled ruefully. "Not yet, I'm just walking in the door," Dex said. "Besides, you know I can't afford real ginger beer. It's just Jamaica's Best and gingapop, but after this bitch of a day, it'll have to do." He griped about his day while at his apartment he poured a couple of fingers of cheap rum into a tumbler and topped it off with ginger ale, watching Annabelle's avatar in the forefront of his vision.

"So, have you been playing?" Annabelle asked.

Dex blushed, but his avatar kept his secret. "Yeah, I've been noodling around a bit. I've been playing all the songs for the next gig, hoping that it won't wreck my virtual mandolin playing."

Dex had recently joined a small pick-up band in M City called Chemical Celeste. He played mandolin, which had been his instrument back in his misspent youth. Playing the virtual instrument was quite different from the real thing, but Dex had picked it up fast and he fit in well with the band. When he was in Europa, Annabelle had surprised him with a gift of a cheap real mandolin. He'd been speechless, but refused to play for her until he had practiced.

Annabelle moved her avatar next to Dex on the banquette seat and leaned in to him. They sat that way for a few minutes in silence and Dex was doing a good job of pretending to like it. "I know you probably aren't going to want to hear this," Dex said, his voice a little thick from the rum, "but I miss you."

Annabelle smiled, a little sadly and squeezed Dex's arm. "It's okay," she said. "I missed you a little when you were in Nice."

Dex controlled the impulse to remind Annabelle that Nice was where she lived and that he had been there only to see her. That they had been together so much more than they were now and that that was what he missed. But he knew she knew that, just like he knew that she craved the times they had at Three Card Monte's or places like it in M City the way he craved being together in the physical world.

He laughed, a tight noise that contained frustration, longing and a strange feeling of hope. "We are some pair, aren't we kiddo?"

Dex saw Annabelle lift her face and he almost felt for a moment like she was really looking into his eyes. "That we are," she said, "that we are."

CHAPTER THREE

THE MAN SAT alone at the bar, looking at the crowd. His avatar looked as if it were simply staring at the row of virtual liquor bottles on the shelf behind the bar, but the man was really scanning the other patrons at the bar carefully. He had his system set to identify the physical location of each person and highlight those who were in the city. There was no point in getting his mind set on someone only to find out that they were actually located halfway around the world.

The bar was reasonably crowded, but no one noticed him sitting on his own. It wasn't unusual to see someone alone in a place like this — its main draw wasn't the company but rather the goods represented by the items behind the bar. This was the finest neural stim joint in M City that the man knew of and he was quite the connoisseur. Though this night he was limiting himself merely to a small dram of focus™, since he was, after all, working.

No one paid him for his work, of course, but he had long ago realized that in this world the truly important work was never properly recognized. He was content now merely to see the work done. He had always found ways to make ends meet some other way. That wasn't important. What was important was what he was doing now.

He scanned the room, automatically looking for the people who were in the city. There weren't many — sometimes he'd spend a whole night in a bar like this and never find a suitable candidate. There were no sure things in this vocation, he knew, and while he would be disappointed if he didn't find someone, it was the way of all things. He was a patient man. He had to be.

He watched as a small group near the door began to get rowdy. They starting singing along with the song that was playing and a few other people at the other end of the bar joined in. He felt a frisson of distaste ripple through his body. Why would they draw such attention to themselves, make themselves so obvious? He had always avoided those stims which contributed to that kind of behaviour. He couldn't understand why anyone would find such a reaction so pleasant it was worth paying for. He felt mortified on their behalf as the song ended and one of their number, a tall, reedy woman, careered around the room. He looked away and sipped his drink, wondering if it were maybe time to cut the night short, when a flash of red caught his peripheral vision.

A woman was entering the bar, her location lit like a beacon. Finally. Someone in the city. Someone he should talk to.

• • •

He had never seen this one before, but that didn't necessarily mean anything. There were a dozen or more places like this that he visited regularly, looking for potential candidates. This woman could be a regular here and he wouldn't know. Or she could be wearing a new body. It didn't matter. He himself used a different avatar every time he worked — it paid to be careful. He watched as the newcomer made her way to the bar and moved his avatar next to hers to eavesdrop on her order. It helped him make his decision if he felt he knew a little something about the possible candidate. This one ordered a particularly powerful cocktail that he knew would make her chatty in a minute or two. Excellent.

She sipped her virtual drink, her avatar's action providing the delivery of the chemical stimulants to the brain. The effects would begin immediately, so he could see no reason to delay. He could feel his heart begin to pound more quickly and was pleased that his avatar would not betray him as easily as his body did.

"Hi," he said, turning to face the woman. He smiled easily and watched as her look of wariness turned quickly to a smile in return. He knew it was the chemicals, not his charm that effected the change, but that didn't matter. "Seems like everywhere you go you hear that song," he continued, jerking his head toward the video screen where a popular band was screeching out their latest hit. "You just can't get away," he said, grinning again.

"Yeah," the woman replied. "It's catchy, though." They chatted idly for about an hour, about nothing of substance. They never even introduced themselves, which was of no consequence since any name he gave would have been false, anyway. In his experience, most of the people who frequented bars like this were interested in anonymity, so there was little point in introductions. When he found suitable candidates, he knew how to learn everything he would need. It would consume him, the need to discover as much as he could about them. The candidate would become the most important person, the most important thing in his life until it was done. But not everyone was a candidate.

He would choose. They were the finest moments in his life, the moments of choice. He could never have explained how he made his choices — he had chosen men, women, people whose gender he'd never known until the very end. Some had turned out to have fashionable bodies, but most were as generic in the physical as his own throwaway avatars were in M City. It had nothing to do with them. It was all about him, his choices. And he had made one now. This woman would die. He smiled at her as she babbled on about some vid she was describing. He looked forward to her end. In the physical world, he fingered the hilt of his knife.

CHAPTER FOUR

DEX BARELY MADE it in to work on time. He and Annabelle had stayed at Monte's until the wee hours and he'd poured himself more than his fair share of refills at his apartment in that time. He'd had to take a shot of Flying Fish Tonix just to get himself moving and he could barely remember the last time he'd been such a mess in the morning. He hoped he wouldn't have another terrible call like the Stiles woman again. He couldn't trust himself not to respond in kind if someone called him a shit-loving meatfucker again.

He rubbed his sore eyes as he logged into the B&B system and caught a glimpse of his neighbour's sour expression turned his way. "Never seen a morning person before, sweetheart?" Dex growled and felt his spirits life slightly as he saw his co-worker's face turn a violent shade of crimson. He didn't even care if the guy told on him. He'd probably make things worse for himself if he did go to management — employees were encouraged to work out internal differences between them on their own. Less work for the suits that way, Dex figured.

Dex ignored the guy he'd started to think of as Mister Mouse and began methodically working his way through his assigned tasks. Days like this made him glad he'd never had any real ambition. A job that really ought to have been done by a half intelligent program instead of poor saps like him was ideal for mornings like this. It was only four drinks, he told himself incredulously. Used to be that he could put away twice that much plus who knew what other pharmaceutical goodies and still perambulate correctly the next day. Dex wondered if maybe it was time he started shelling out for higher quality food bricks. He didn't expect the old meat sack to start giving in already.

At lunch, he headed for the break room and his third cup of the swill B&B served as coffee. He looked up and, surprised, saw an old deskmate standing by the machine.

"Heya, Dex," the woman said, leaning up against the counter. "Haven't seen you in a while."

Dex looked at her and smiled. They had gotten on much better than he did with Mister Mouse and he hadn't realized how much he had missed her. "Jeez, Hazel," Dex said, "it's got to be an age since you moved up to the sales floor. What are you doing down here with us schlubs? It can't be the gourmet java we brew down here." He grimaced and shoved his large mug under the spigot. Hazel watched the brown water pour into Dex's cavernous cup and laughed.

"Sales is a harsh master, but they don't remove our taste buds," she said. "All the meeting rooms upstairs were booked, so they sent us down here for the day." She pointed at Dex's cup. "How can you drink that stuff?"

Dex took a sip and wrinkled his nose. "It's not so bad if you don't smell it," he said. "Besides, on mornings like this, I need something to stop me from going on a rampage. Or falling asleep on my desk."

Hazel laughed again. "I hear you loud and clear on that one." She leaned in toward him and said, "If you're really desperate, I can drop some Lightning on you."

Dex raised an eyebrow. "Hazel, you rebel, you. I never would have suspected." She shushed him, even though they were alone and both of them were well aware that performance enhancing stimulants were expressly permitted by B&B's drug policy. "No thanks," Dex said. "I prefer to suffer."

"That suits you," Hazel said, smiling. "Anyway, I've got to get back to the world's most boring staff meeting. It was good to see you again, Dex."

"Yeah, you too, Hazel." She turned to walk out of the break room, but stopped and turned back to face Dex.

"You know," she said, "if you hadn't said anything, I never would have known."

"Known what?" Dex asked.

Hazel laughed. "You just look pretty good for a rough morning, that's all. What happened to you in the last six months?" Dex felt his face flush and he mumbled something. "Oh, it's none of my business, I know," Hazel said. "I'm just happy to see it. Whatever it is, don't stop doing it." She turned and left the break room.

• • •

When Dex got back to his desk, he started on a couple of tasks and then activated his surreptitious program to access everywherenet without his bosses knowing what he was up to. He pinged Annabelle, just wanting to hear her voice. She answered after a long pause and before Dex could say anything, said, "That's the last time I let you keep me out past my bed time. What a day I'm having! I'm working with this team in Namerica and the one person I need couldn't be bothered to show up today. And I have a head-ache. And I haven't had enough sleep. You are a bad influence, Mister Dexter. A very bad influence, indeed."

Dex laughed and saw his desk neighbour try to hide a disgusted look. Dex was subvocalizing, so Mister Mouse wasn't eavesdropping exactly, but Dex was sure that the smartass was well aware that he wasn't on a client call. He didn't care. Maybe getting shitcanned from this job wouldn't be so bad. To Annabelle, he said, "And I'm sure you were just little miss "early to bed, early to rise" before you hoodwinked me into keeping time with you, is that it?"

"Hoodwinked!" Annabelle said, mock appalled. "I'm not even sure what that word means. Where did you get your dictionary, an antique store?"

"Verily," Dex replied and smiled as Annabelle chuckled. "Anyway, I was just calling to remind you of the gig tomorrow night. The Dog and Pony bar, in Chandlers. You'll be there?"

"Wouldn't miss it for all the beauty sleep in the world," Annabelle answered and Dex couldn't help but grin.

"I'll see you there, then," he said and ended the call.

• • •

After he'd let slip to Annabelle that he used to be a musician, she wheedled him into trying the virtual mandolin. He had been apprehensive, for many reasons. But as much as Dex still felt out of place and uncomfortable in the virtual world, he had found a surprisingly large amount of pleasure in playing the fake instrument. Remembering his old bands, he wondered if it were possible to find the same joy in playing with others in M City as he had back in the hovels of the streets. After weeks of badgering by Annabelle, his curiosity finally got the better of him and he went to an open jam session one night.

It had been very strange and not entirely in a pleasant way. But Dex could hear the music they were making together just as well through his implants as he had once heard live music with his ears. And while he would be the first to admit that playing a program with virtual bandmates was nowhere near as good as the real thing, it was a fine substitute. He went back the next week and at the end of the evening, Javier, one of the keyboardists who had been playing with Dex, asked him if he'd be willing to play in a band a night or two a month. Talking to Javier, Dex found himself getting excited in a way he thought he'd never feel again. Of course, he said yes.

This was going to be Chemical Celeste's first show since Dex joined. He was nervous and happy and a little sad. Every time he played with the band it reminded him of his old friends and the life he had lost. When he tried to remember why he had given it all up, the memories of scrounging for food and a place to live and always being on the fringes of society had a romantic tinge to them. He mentally shook his head, reminding himself that everyone has to grow up sometime. He'd started to do it when he got his first real job and with it some measure of responsibility. Also, a real apartment, more disposable cash than he'd ever seen before and a taste for cheap rum.

Dex had had many low rank jobs over the years. His current position was not terribly good, though he had been with the firm long enough that he got a few perks that most CSRs didn't receive. He knew, from the few conversations with his neighbours, that his own building was populated with mainly sales staff, who were at least one rung higher on the corporate ladder than support staff. Even so, he knew all about the problems of underemployment.

There was very little in life that was not tied to employment — pay, of course, but also housing, law enforcement, even funeral arrangements. If, of course, you died while still working or had a good 'retirement' package. What a laughable euphemism that was. The only thing in most retirement packages was a room in a convalescent institution and a plan to get rid of your corpse. Dex was only in his sixties, so worrying about that time of life was seventy or eighty years off at least. It still pissed him off.

Back at his apartment that evening, he thought about the notice he's seen at the organization's news board that morning. Pat Malone, the head of the part of the organization known as the goon squad, was retiring. Everyone who came into the organization started in the goons, who took care of the rough and tumble aspect of the streets. They broke up fights, kept a kind of order in the worse neighbourhoods and were the first line of contact for the organization. Malone had been a lifer among the goons — there were always a few who really shone there. He'd risen to the role of lieutenant, a title that meant little in the organization other than a mark of respect and a vague indication of responsibilities.

Dex had always liked Malone, though they had never really worked together and spoken rarely. Dex had no idea Malone was so old, but the notice had been clear. Malone was leaving the squad, leaving the organization and going into retirement. Everyone knew that meant he would probably soon be dead. It made Dex sad and he made a note to remind himself to get Malone something nice for his going away party. Dex wondered what the man liked to drink.

CHAPTER FIVE

DEX WAS EARLY to The Dog and Pony. There were only three other people there — Javier and a woman friend of his and Annabelle. "We don't go on for another hour," he said to her, after enduring her virtual embrace. "What are you doing here already?"

"I just couldn't wait to see you," she said, the corners of her lips turned up in a grin. She looked him over and giggled when she noticed his flaming crimson tie, which stood out from his dark pin-striped suit like a bloodstain on a sheet. "I remember that," she said, running her fingers along its length. Dex flushed in real life and his avatar even managed to look embarrassed without changing colour.

"Well, if it was good enough for you, it should be good enough for them," Dex gestured at the empty seats at the tables in the small cabaret.

"You'll knock 'em dead, honey," Annabelle said, winking. "See, you're not the only one who can hit up the antiquarian dictionary market." She moved to a table near the front and sat. Dex noticed that he wasn't the only one who had spent some time in the wardrobe. Annabelle had done herself up for the evening, too. Her hair came just below her earlobes and where it was usually a light brown it was now a luminescent deep gold colour. It didn't just catch and reflect the light at the bar, but it created its own glow. It set off the almost violet eyes she was wearing very nicely. She wore a simple cream coloured dress, which in a virtual world where half the denizens wore wings or horns as accessories, stood out more than a glittered gown ever would have. Dex had not been won over by Annabelle's looks, either in the virtual or the physical worlds, but he admitted to himself that he was proud to be seen with her.

Slowly the rest of the band trickled in — Suzi on the trumpet, Arvind on the drum kit and Kandace on the mixer. They joked around nervously; Dex knew that for all of them except himself and Javier, this was the first time they would have played for a real audience. Javier was giving a warm up talk while he set up his keyboards. "I'm not going to pretend that this isn't a big deal, because it is. Playing for a crowd isn't the same as jamming or playing for your friends. The audience is part it, the vibe they give you will influence your playing. Don't try to fight it, but don't over think it, either. You're all good enough. Just play."

They all grinned at each other as they finished getting their virtual instruments set up on the small stage. Dex knew that, like him, they were all busy setting up their programs in their apartments, probably alone, maybe even in their pajamas. Even he found it easy to forget his real surroundings, as he watched the virtual bar slowly fill with people. They took their places on the stage and the lights dimmed slightly. A disembodied voice, that Dex was fairly certain was a program, announced the name of the band. As the voice said the first syllable of 'Celeste', Arvind gave a quick "one, two, three, four," and they started to play.

There were a few missed cues in the first song, but the audience didn't seem to mind. By the time they were finishing the first set, they were tight and in the groove. The small space filled with applause as they left the stage, each of them buzzing with the thrill. Dex sat across from Annabelle, who had acquired another three people at the table. Dex recognized Evan and Fredrick, a couple of Annabelle's friends that Dex had met a few times before in M City.

He thanked them for coming, then looked over and saw that the fourth person at the small table was Zahara Zhang, his squad captain. "Zizou," Dex said, using the captain's nickname and sounding a little flummoxed. "I didn't think anyone on the squad knew about this." He shot Annabelle a look.

His captain grinned. "As far as I know, they don't," she said. "I had no idea it was you playing tonight. I just come here every Thursday for the bands." She took a sip of her drink. "You were pretty good. I'm glad to see you aren't wasting your talent."

"Thanks, Cap," Dex said, looking sheepishly at Annabelle.

"I'll drink to that," she said, smiling at Dex. "Here's to making use of what you've got."

"To realizing potential," Evan said, lifting his virtual beer bottle and the others raised their glasses to the centre of the table.

• • •

After the second set, Dex had a drink with the band and Annabelle said goodbye to her friends who were leaving and joined Dex and the others. Zahara Zhang stopped by briefly to compliment the band, then left. "See you two tomorrow," she said as she walked out of the bar, reminding Dex and Annabelle of the weekly squad meeting. Annabelle couldn't stop grinning, her arm linked with Dex's as the musicians conducted a happy post-mortem on the gig.

After they were done, Dex and Annabelle walked out of the bar and strolled arm in arm down the streets of Chandlers. Most people linked directly into and out of specific locations in M City, but some areas were decorated well enough outside the rooms and buildings that there were always some folks just walking around. Chandlers was one of those neighbourhoods and Dex was more comfortable on its dark, lamplit streets than he was anywhere in the virtual world. Annabelle had become a wanderer herself in recent months, looking for any way for both of them to be happy when they were together.

"You look like the cat that got the bird," Dex said, after they'd walked about a block.

"What does that mean?" Annabelle asked, still grinning.

"So you haven't memorized my dictionary yet," Dex said. "I mean you look smug, like you just cracked into the most secure system on the 'nets, made off with a virtual suitcase full of cash and twenty-three priceless secrets and no one is the wiser."

"Oh," Annabelle said. "You mean, why do I look happy? Can't I just be enjoying a night out with a handsome and talented man? Does something have to be up just because I'm happy?"

"Nice try, kiddo," Dex said, smiling. "You've got the look. Spill it."

Annabelle laughed and squeezed Dex's arm. "I'm just still kind of amazed that you really did it. Playing with the band and everything, here, like a regular person." Dex couldn't stop his reaction in time and Annabelle felt him go stiff. "Oh, shit," she said, stopping and turning to face him. "I'm sorry. I didn't mean it like that. I mean, it's not like I'm exactly normal myself."

"I know what you meant," Dex said, dropping her hand and stepping back. "And you're right, it was a big step for me tonight. And I never would have done it without you. But you must know that it's not easy for me. None of this is. It's getting better all the time, but I still feel like a fraud here." He gestured around him at the street, but Annabelle knew that he was referring to M City, to the virtual world which was the only place where she felt like a complete person.

"It's real," she said, certainty making her voice hard. "What we have is real, no matter how hard it is for us to be together. You know it is, Dex. I know you feel what I feel, or you wouldn't be here."

"You're right," Dex said, looking past Annabelle. "If I didn't feel it, I wouldn't be doing any of this." He looked at her, then looked away again. "But wanting to be with you so much and knowing you want to be with me, then having to settle for — this." He spat the last word out like it was rotten. He felt a lump form in his throat and he choked it back. "It's hard," he simply said, finally.

Annabelle looked up at Dex's eyes, the eyes she saw in her mind when she imagined him. Eyes that were darker, more uniform than physical eyes could ever be. She never thought of Dex's physical body, only his avatar. Even when they were together in the physical world, where he was finally comfortable, Annabelle still imagined the virtual man when she struggled to endure his touch. "This is just as hard for me," she said, her voice cracking. She felt Dex's avatar touch her cheek, the sensation soothing and sensual and heartbreaking.

"I know it is, kiddo," Dex said. They stood like that for a moment, two representations of people appearing to face each other in the dim simulated glow of a streetlight, their real bodies separated by one ocean of water and another of incompatible desire.

CHAPTER SIX

THE MAN WOKE early, the sound of his roommate in the lav startling him out of sleep against his will. He never bothered to set his system with an alarm, since Gerry was always up early, always in the lav first thing in the morning. He would never have chosen to live with a man like Gerry — there was nothing wrong with him, but they had nothing in common, nothing to talk about. At least he didn't get upset or ask any questions when the man was out at night. It could have been worse.

After Gerry left for his shift, the man cleaned himself and ate, then walked to the train stop and rode the forty minutes to the factory. He had forgotten how he'd even gotten this job. This job was like all the others he'd had all his life — something that he just fell into. His jobs were always crummy — he had no formal training and wasn't burly enough to get work as a roughneck or labourer in the physical world. This one wasn't that bad; the work was easy, his apartment was fine and even his roommate was tolerable. He'd had worse, certainly.

The man sat at his workstation, running tests on the new equipment. He was just putting each device in the machine, pressing a button and checking the readouts. It wasn't a real test, not like if he put the tiny metallic tube up to his face and thumbed it on. He guessed someone else got to do that, someone who didn't work in this dark basement for a tiny shared apartment and just enough for food. He wouldn't have minded that job — these new Joybuzzers were supposed to deliver anything from a mild sense of well-being to orgasmic rapture with just a few milliamps. Better than stims, the marketing people said, though the man didn't believe anything they said.

One of the few perks of his job was that he got a good discount, so he'd used Joybuzzers plenty, on himself as well as on others. The model just before this one was pretty good — the sting didn't last long and the feelings were intense, but he always found the sensation to be more external than he would have liked. It always felt like something was being done to him, which of course, it was. But with stims, the feeling came from the inside out, as if you made it yourself, as if it were natural. You always knew with the 'buzzers that it was something that was given to you. And things that you were given could be taken away.

He often thought about things like this while he performed his tests. He was really just a button masher — he often wondered why they even bothered using people for such dull work. He supposed it must just be cheaper to employ him to put the tubes in the testing machine and turn it on than it would be to make a robot. And there were no maintenance costs. When he broke down, he would just be replaced. At one time a thought like that would have filled him with a blinding rage. Now, it just made him chuckle. It was amazing the things that stop seeming important once you have a purpose to your life.

A purpose. That was something he definitely had now. It made him think of the woman from the stim bar. He wished he were with her now, with his knife and his plan, instead of at this workstation, pushing buttons like a drone. He toyed with the small tube in his hand and wondered how expensive these new 'buzzers were. The last candidate had had some expensive upgrades that had come out during the process and the man had managed to sell them at one of those places in brown sector. He'd gotten a little cash out of the sale and he thought he ought to reinvest it. These new 'buzzers were much less bulky than the one he used now and they were supposed to give an even greater level of pleasure. He had no desire to cause pain. That wasn't his purpose.

After the shift he would see about getting a new 'buzzer. He wondered if he could trade in his old model for an even bigger discount. He couldn't count on the candidates having parts worth selling and even with his discount the 'buzzers were expensive. But he was a frugal man and he didn't need much. A little went a long way with him and he could probably swing a new tool every once in a while. He was careful with his tools. He would sharpen the knife that evening. He used an old whetstone and it took a long time to keep the edge right. But it was good work, better than pushing a button all day. And while he honed the edge he would decide when he would take her. When his work would begin.

CHAPTER SEVEN

DEX LINKED IN to the meeting just as the roll call was getting started. He was never a lover of meetings and the weekly meeting was an unnecessary chore, but he had to admit to himself that he had grown to like the camaraderie of the group. He preferred to work alone and usually he did, but over the years he had come to rely on the other men and women in the squad. You don't spend significant portions of your time with a group of people without making a few pals.

Squad captain Zahara Zhang checked attendance quickly and asked Pat Malone about one of his people who wasn't present. "Vonruden?" the captain asked.

"Conflict with the day job," Malone replied. "I'll fill her in later." The captain nodded sharply and began the meeting. The first item on the agenda was a report from Malone about the week's activities on the goon squad. Street fights and muggings didn't usually have much to do with Dex's cases, but he found the work interesting. Usually there wasn't much to report from the street team, so Dex's ears perked up. He had enjoyed his time as a goon and no one was more surprised than he when he ended up as a detective. Even now he missed the rush of walking the streets, dealing with people face to fleshy face, the visceral realness of blood and sweat and skin.

"There's the usual petty stuff," Malone said, after the captain gave him the floor. "A bit of a decrease in stupid violence since the stim bar in brown sector shut down last month. But the interesting thing is this..." Malone sent everyone a small file with a brief written report and some images. "We found a body in one of those abandoned buildings in brown."

"One of the buildings the squatters have been using?" Jay Shiraishi, Malone's second in command, asked.

"No," Malone said. "It's that derelict one that's missing a wall, on the south side of Simcoe Street." There were nods of recognition among the street team. Malone continued. "There is a small room in the interior of the building that is actually intact on all sides. A stimmed out streeter was poking around in there looking for a nest when he found it. We got the call pretty quick and I don't think anyone touched anything."

"So some malnourished streeter just found a little hidey hole to curl up and die in?" Shiraishi asked again.

"Take a look at the file, Jay," Malone said, not bothering to hide his annoyance. "Last I checked, it takes more than missing a meal or two to lose huge strips of skin like that." With that there was a long pause as everyone opened the file Malone had sent.

"Jesus Christ," a voice near the back of the room said. "What the fuck happened there?"

"Tests on the scene indicate that this guy died of loss of blood. There was quite a lot of blood on the scene and you don't take off that much skin without spilling a drop of two. We also found marks on the deceased's wrists which indicate that he had been restrained at some point and there were small traces of polymer rope found at the scene."

"We're treating it as a possible homicide," Captain Zhang said.

"Possible?" someone exclaimed incredulously. Malone whipped around to the sound of the voice.

"It's possible that this was a consensual thing," Malone said. "If you look closely you'll see that the deceased has a big grin on his face and we found elevated levels of endorphins and dopamine in his system."

"A stim junkie?" Dex asked, drawn in to the case along with the rest of the squad.

"Doesn't look like it," Malone said. "The drugs were all naturally occurring. There was none of the telltale branding of commercial neurostims and home brew uppers look totally different to the sniffers than the real things. We're thinking either direct node stimulation or this guy really got off on being flayed."

Dex could hear several people murmuring. "Jesus," someone said and another person said, astonished, "It takes all kinds to make a world, I guess."

"Enough chatter," Zahara Zhang said and everyone shut up. "Malone's people are on this for now, until we determine who this guy is. Chances are some firm's Security team will take over from there. Now, in other news, there's the big ugly house. Annabelle, an update?"

Annabelle had been working on trying to determine the rightful owner of a piece of virtual property in M City. This kind of case had become the bread and butter of the organization, now that so many people used the virtual world as their primary recreation area. Businesses were flourishing there and an entire underground economy had been created. Outside the sphere of influence of the firms, there were no private Security forces in M City, so the Cubicle Men found plenty of work among the avatar designers, virtual hookers and gambling houses.

The house in question was indeed sprawling and of a design that most people would have guessed issued from the mind of an architect well pickled by an intense and expensive cocktail of drugs, but was described by critics as incomprehensible genius. It was used as part night club, part brothel by one of M City's most successful entrepreneurs, Anthony O'Rourke. The trouble was that O'Rourke hadn't designed the big ugly house himself; he had bought the plans from a designer named Tisha Chiou and had the thing created from those specs. The designer was now trying to argue that the plans were merely leased to O'Rourke and that the actual look of the thing still belonged to her. Chiou wouldn't have had a leg to stand on, except that O'Rourke used images of the house in his advertisements and a tiny version of the thing was his corporate logo. Chiou argued that O'Rourke was entitled to one instance of the big ugly house and that was it. She had hired Annabelle to find a way to prove that O'Rourke had overstepped the limits of his license.

"I've been going through the code for the logo, trying to find something that proves that it's just a copy of Chiou's design," Annabelle reported. "O'Rourke's people are clever; they've stripped out all the obvious stuff, but I've come across several indicators. There's a particular syntax that Chiou uses for doorways and while it isn't unique, it is unusual." Zahara Zhang's face had the blank look avatars get when the person behind them has stopped paying attention and she was sure no one else was listening either, so Annabelle pressed on quickly. "Anyway, I think I'm a day or two away from having enough to go after O'Rourke."

"Good," the captain said, snapping back into action. She spent the next few minutes rounding up the other outstanding cases, then said, "And, finally, I have something for you Dex." He perked up his head and felt his heart rate pick up a little. He'd been riding the pine for too long, he felt, nothing coming up for him since the Velasquez case. Dex was ready for a new puzzle to solve. He felt his head grow heavy as the new case file downloaded to his system and he opened up the summary file. He scanned it quickly, then refocussed on the squad room.

"There must be some mistake," he said, already sure that there was, in fact, no mistake at all, seeing the smirk on the captain's face. "This is a case for the Housing Bureau or something, not for us."

"There is no Housing Bureau," the captain said, the smile on her face widening. "These people are living in terrible conditions and they've tried everything they can to get their employer to fix them without success. They are out of options, so they've come to us. That's what we're here for and everyone has to take a turn — even on the more mundane cases." Dex sighed and closed his eyes. He tried not to sound like a petulant child and almost succeeded.

"But this is a compensation and benefits issue," he said. "What am I supposed to do about internal policies at..." he scanned the file again, looking for the name of his clients' employer, "at Aspertech?"

"You figure it out," the captain said, "that's why you get the big bucks."

Dex sighed again and said, "Other than the complainants quitting their jobs and looking for something else with better digs, I'm kind of at a loss as to how to help them."

"Well," the captain said, "you're not getting another assignment until you close out this one, so hopefully that will motivate you to use some of your legendary creativity to find a solution." She grinned at Dex, whose avatar scowled while his real cheeks burned in embarrassment. "Okay, people," the captain said. "That's all I have this week. Off you go to your bitch sessions."

Most of the squad met after the meetings in one of the bars in Chandlers for drinks and bonding. These unofficial meetings were where most of the real work got done — favours and information were bartered between rounds. The goon squad tended to stick together at Sally's Slipper, a rough honkytonk where they could easily knock back several neurostim enhanced drinks, get a little rowdy and still be welcomed back the following week.

Pat Malone wasn't one of the regulars at Sally's Slipper. The lieutenant didn't hold his rank over the other members of the goons, but he knew that his role was different from theirs. He knew that the goons needed to bond with each other and that sometimes that would be at his expense. He was a social man, though, so he would often tag along with the detectives to Three Card Monte's after the meeting. He caught Dex's eye after the captain had dismissed the squad. "You going to Monte's?" he asked.

Dex said, "After that tongue lashing, I figure I should just get home and figure out something to do with that housing thing."

The lieutenant grinned. "She's just yanking your chain. Come on," he said, "I'll stand you a round and even give you and idea or two on this case."

"Well, there's an offer I can't refuse," Dex said. "But why all the help all of a sudden?"

"Let's just say that you probably won't be getting something for nothing." The two men linked out of the meeting room and found themselves watching a smoky, dark bar materialize around them. "You grab a table," Malone said, "and I'll get us a couple of drinks. What works for you?"

"Rum and ginger," Dex said. "Au natural."

"Suit yourself," the older man said and went off in search of a free bartender.

Chapter Eight

WHILE MALONE WAS gone, Dex looked through the notes on his new case. The six clients had been complaining to their benefits manager for over a year about the conditions in their apartment complex. The benefits clerk, one Wendell Burstein, had replied to each complaint with the same bureaucratic bullshit: "The units in the building located at 175 Massey Drive are within the prescribed parameters for employees of your rank. Your request for reassignment is denied." Dex hated Wendell Burstein already.

He looked though the details of the complaints and began to get even more angry. His own apartment was small, there was no denying that. Just one room, with a narrow bed at one end, a small table and chair and cupboards and a zapper along one wall. His lav was big enough, though, and the water was always hot and the dryer worked just fine. He actually liked this apartment better than all the others he'd been allocated at his various jobs. Maybe it was a perk of seniority or maybe his tastes were just getting more modern.

His clients, though, truly were living in a terrible hovel. There were six of them who had come to the Cubicle Men looking for help. They all worked for Aspertech, a giant firm whose name was on everything from clothes to water to maglev train cars. The six of them shared three rooms in one of Aspertech's buildings. Each room was hardly larger than Dex's own apartment and that was where the similarities ended. The lavs were tiny and there was only water half the time. The dryers put out barely a puff of air, so when they did have water they had to dry themselves on towels, which they could never seem to get clean in the broken-down autoclaves in the rooms. The zappers barely worked and the doors barely closed. They also complained that the sprinklers and locking systems were always malfunctioning.

They were the kind of terrible conditions that Dex expected to find in the dilapidated old private buildings that people without any housing benefits at all had to live in, not in a building owned by a firm like Aspertech. He thought back to his youth, when he was still trying to be a starving artist, playing music in grimy physical world bars and living in dumps. He wasn't sure he'd ever lived anywhere as bad as his poor Aspertech clients. There was no doubt that it was a boring assignment, but Dex was starting to feel like he might have a good time hassling Aspertech about this.

• • •

Pat Malone returned with a small tumbler for Dex and a beer for himself. He sat opposite Dex at the small table and slid the rum and ginger across the tabletop. The program for the bar simulation created the look of a wet slick where the sweating glass appeared to have passed over the table. Dex picked up the glass and raised it in a silent toast to the goon squad lieutenant. Malone smiled, returning the salute, and took a long pull on his beer.

"Ah," he sighed after swallowing. "I've never met a beer I didn't like. Even so," he gestured at the virtual glass, "this stuff can't hold a candle to the real thing. That's why my big farewell shindig is going to be out there. There's this fellow I know who brews his own ale and runs a pub down in green sector. It will be nice to finally really meet you mucky mucks."

Dex smiled. It was a shame Malone was on his way out — Dex was beginning to really like the old man. "So, Pat," Dex said, "you said you might be able to point me in the right direction with this housing problem."

"I've helped a few people out with a similar kind of thing, though it's not usually a corporate apartment, if you know what I mean." Dex nodded and took a sip of his drink. "It depends on what your clients want to get out of it and what they can afford, both in money and hassle."

"I only scanned the notes," Dex admitted, "so I'm not sure what their agenda is. Why don't you lay it all on me and I can take it from there?"

"Okay," Malone said and took another drink of his beer. The frosty pint glass was about half empty now. "If they just want the deficiencies fixed, that's the easiest. I know a couple of folks who can fix just about anything and they are pretty cheap about it." Malone lowered his voice, even though their conversation had been on a private channel all the time they'd been at the table. It wasn't just the atmosphere which drew the detectives to Three Card Monte's, it was the various private and encrypted channels available for use there. "They've got a printer."

Dex let out a breath. Printers had been hard to come by his whole life, after one of the major firms had managed to win a patent suit against the much smaller manufacturers. The official story was that all printers had been destroyed, but everyone knew it wasn't true. Even so, Dex had never seen anything that had been made by a printer, as far as he knew, and he'd certainly never seen an actual printer.

"Isn't that a bit risky?" he asked Malone. "I mean, these clients of ours are really an unknown quantity — who's to say that they don't see a bigger payoff in turning these guys of yours in."

"That's where you come in," Malone said, grinning. "Your clients don't need to know who's fixing the problems or how. You just tell them how much it costs and arrange for the work to get done. Problem solved."

"Okay," Dex said. "What if they can't even afford your guys? Or they really want to stick it to their employer?"

"Well, that gets a lot more tricky," Malone said, frowning. "You'd need to start by getting a copy of their employment contract, the long one. Housing arrangements will be spelled out in there. If it turns out that the conditions of their apartments are consistent with what's in the contract, they're screwed. Otherwise, they have to try and prove breach of contract and that's tricky. Especially because then their employer is going to go over their records with a magnifier, looking for anything they could use as breach of contract against them. They could just as easily lose their jobs as get the lavs fixed."

"That's pretty much what I guessed," Dex said. "At least I've got a second opinion on it now. As much as I'd really like to take these Aspertech bastards down a peg or two, I think I'll give them the hard sell on just fixing the problem and dropping the complaint."

"It's a shitty deal," Malone said, polishing off his beer. "That's one of the good things about this gig — you might get stuck at a lousy job with a crappy employer, but you've got enough extra cash to make the rest of your life decent."

"And if the job's really terrible," Dex added, "you can always leave and the Men will find something else."

"We got it good here, my man," Malone said. "We're definitely the lucky ones."

"Amen," Dex said, as a smouldering cigarette materialized between his fingers. He brought it to his lips, inhaled and then shot out a plume of blue smoke.

Malone gestured at the smoke. "Is that delivering, or just for looks?" "Just looks," Dex admitted. "I don't really like neurostims. I'm more of your fifth of cheap rum kind of guy."

"Yeah," Malone said. "That's what I figured. But I didn't figure you for the accessorized type."

Dex smiled, but there was little warmth to it. "Me neither," he said. "Things change, though. Sometimes you have to be willing to change along with them."

Malone's face grew dark. "And sometimes you don't get the choice."

Dex thought about the other man's imminent retirement. "I'm sorry, Pat," he said, genuinely.

"It's what it is," the older man said, then his face changed back to its usual jovial look. "Where has that pretty lass of yours got herself to? You'll both be coming to my big party, I trust."

"I wouldn't miss it," Dex said. "It might be tough for Annabelle, though. She's physically in Europa."

"What?" Malone asked. "Holiday?"

"No," Dex said. "She lives there. In Nice."

"What's she doing on our squad, then?"

"She lived here when she first joined up," Dex said. "Her day job moved her to Nice, but her hours are still on Pac time, so she never transferred. She's a cracker; all her work is done online, so it really doesn't matter where she is."

Malone grunted. "Must matter now, though," he said. "The two of you..."

Dex ground his cigarette out on the heel of his shoe and dropped the end. It disappeared before it hit the floor. "It's difficult," he said, not looking at Malone. Before he had to say any more, Annabelle joined them at the table.

"Well, speak of the devil," Malone said, smiling broadly. "Dex here was just telling me that a little thing like the Atlantic ocean was going to stop you from coming to my retirement party."

"Oh, I think I can find a way over that," Annabelle said, looking at Dex. "I'm willing to put myself out a little for something important."

Dex looked at her face, which had hardened into an unusually serious expression. He reached across the table and took her hand. "Thanks, Pat," he said to Malone. "For the help with my case."

Malone smiled and Dex thought he could catch a little trace of sadness in the look. "Always did like helping out my fellow man," he said. "And I think with that I shall be off and leave the night to you young ones." He stood and Dex reached over to shake the man's hand.

"See you at the party," Dex said.

"I'll hold you to that," Malone said, then winking at Annabelle, he linked out of the bar.

• • •

"You're really going to come all this way for Malone's party?" Dex asked, incredulous.

"It's on my weekend," Annabelle said, "and I can afford the flight. Besides, it will give us an extra couple of days together. I thought that would make you happy."

"It does," Dex said, "oh, it does. But you're going to hate it. There will probably be maybe fifty people at this thing. How are you going to handle it?"

"I don't know, Dex," Annabelle said, her voice thick. "But I'm going to try. I really am trying to make this work, you know. You aren't the only one who is sacrificing here. Besides, I like Pat Malone a lot. He's a lot like you, I think. And I'm sad to see him go and I want to be there. For him, not just for you."

Dex didn't know what to say. "Should I book your usual room?" he asked, trying to keep his voice light. Annabelle thought a moment.

"Yes," she said, softly. "I'd really like to stay with you..." Her voice trailed off. "Well, what I'd really like is to really want to stay with you. But I'm not quite there yet." She looked away. "I'm sorry."

"Me, too," Dex said and squeezed her avatar's hand.

CHAPTER NINE

DEX WAS STARTING to wonder if he had done something horrible to mornings in the past and they were now out for revenge. His head pounded and his mouth tasted like something had died in it. What had he done last night? He remembered the squad meeting and his chat with Pat Malone after — and then the conversation with Annabelle. And the two large tumblers of rum he'd had after he logged out of M City. Had he eaten anything? He couldn't remember.

He grabbed the bottle of Flying Fish that he'd had the presence of mind to leave beside the bed and took a healthy swig. As soon as the viscous liquid hit his stomach, he started to feel better. Or at least well enough to get out of bed. He managed to shower and get a bite of a food brick in him and decided that he could possibly face the day. He dressed and headed out of his building to the train stop.

He got to his desk, grinned evilly at Mister Mouse and looked forward to another boring day at the office. Working with a hangover was one of the perks of a dull job — he was just at the right mental state for his work when his head pounded and he could barely think. Is that how the rest of them get through the days, he wondered. He slowly and methodically began his work day.

He even read the internal news bulletin. Word for word, unlike his usual quick scan if he bothered to opened the thing. He later wondered if he'd even have noticed the piece if he hadn't been in such a rough shape. It was buried a couple of paragraphs down, after some junk about a new food brick supplier for the canteen. Hazel Ramer was missing.

Missing? Dex had just talked to her the other day. Apparently, she had missed work the previous day and the logs from her apartment showed that she hadn't been back since the day Dex had seen her. She hadn't taken anything from her apartment and there was no activity on her bank accounts. The post asked people to come forward if they saw her or knew anything, but it was just a formality. They must think she was gone for good, Dex thought. They wouldn't want to start a rumour of an opening in sales if they thought she was coming back.

He had a bad feeling about it. Dex knew plenty of people over the years who just stopped turning up one day. He'd even done it once himself at a truly terrible job when he found something better. Dex knew Hazel didn't love sales, but he also knew she didn't hate it. Or at least she didn't hate it enough to just fly without even taking her stuff from her apartment. He hadn't really known her very well, but this seemed out of character.

He wondered about her offer of pharmaceutical assistance. Did that have something to do with it, Dex wondered. He's seen plenty of cases of people who got hooked on stims and let everything else slide. He didn't think it was an overnight kind of thing and Hazel had seemed fine the other day. But you never really know what's going on in another person's head.

Dex realized that his own head was only throbbing dully now. If he'd found a hangover cure in discovering that a pal was missing, he wouldn't be patenting that one. He'd take the pain any day. He started in on his tasks, mindlessly knocking things off his assignment sheet, thinking instead about Hazel. Later, he would poke through the Cubicle Men's files and see if he could find anything out. Zizou had warned Dex that he wouldn't be assigned another case until the housing problem was cleared, but surely she wouldn't stop him from investigating Hazel's disappearance. At least, a little bit.

• • •

By the time Dex got home, he was starting to think that he was spending too much time being a detective and was seeing foul play where there was only impulsiveness. He scanned the identity chip embedded in his hand over the door to his apartment and heard the click of the lock sliding open. He stepped into his small apartment and locking the door behind him, undressed. He stuffed his ugly B&B uniform in the autoclave and stepped into the shower. It would be his second of the day, which meant that he'd have to skip a day this month or fork over some cash for an extra hot water ration. Either way, he didn't care right at that moment. He needed the hot water to clear his head.

He stood under the hot spray, rubbing his soapy cloth roughly over his body. He leaned against the steel wall of the lav and let the two minutes of water pound his body. He didn't even move when the shower head shut the flow off and began emitting a powerful warm jet of air. He let the blower dry him and the room, then padded back into his apartment. He couldn't shake the feeling that something terrible had happened to Hazel Ramer, but he also knew that there wouldn't be any information for him to look at yet. He grabbed a food brick from the large box labelled Econoline next to the zapper and poured a glass of water. Still naked from his shower, he sat on the edge of his bed, alternately swigging from the water glass and taking great bites of the food bar.

Dex was still sitting there ten minutes later, an empty water glass and food brick wrapper in his hand, trying to figure out why he had this sudden desire to pour a shot of rum and rummage through his old video collection, when he felt rather than heard a chime in his head. He blinked his eyes a few times and thought the sequence required to answer the call. It was Annabelle.

"Just checking up on you," she said, her voice light and sunny as usual. "See how you're doing after another grueling day in the salt mines."

"Actually," Dex said, "it was a shitter of a day."

"What happened?" Annabelle asked.

Dex ran a hand over his bald head, feeling the slight stubble under his fingers. "Possibly nothing," Dex said. "I don't want to talk about it yet until I know what's going on."

"Are you okay?" Annabelle asked, concern heavy in her voice.

"Sure, kiddo," Dex said. "It's just something at work. I'll tell you about it some other time. Look, I've got to get started on that housing thing, or I'll never get it done. I'll talk to you tomorrow, okay?"

"Um, sure," Annabelle said. "Look, about last night —"

"There's nothing to say about last night," Dex said, trying to keep his fatigue and frustration out of his voice. "None of this is new for us. I'm sorry if I'm being difficult; I'm really tired these days and I just need a bit of time to get back on track. But we are still good, kiddo, I promise. Just give me a little room, okay?" He heard Annabelle sigh, as if her lips were right next to his ear rather than thousands of klicks away.

"Okay," she said. "But don't take too long, or I'll have to go back to stalking you."

Dex laughed. "I'll do my best not to inconvenience you."

"Good," Annabelle said, mock seriously. "Talk to you tomorrow," she said and broke the connection.

Dex refilled his water glass and threw on an old one piece that he would never be seen in public wearing. He sat at his table and opened his notes from his conversation with Pat Malone. He spent the next hour drafting a proposition for his clients that would get at least some of their complaints addressed. When he finished, he sent copies to each of his clients and filed one in the Cubicle Men's system. After that, he logged out of everywherenet and went to the small cupboard over the water tap. He eyed the bottle of Jamaica's Best for a while, then closed the cupboard door and went to bed. Even without pharmacological help, he was asleep within minutes.

CHAPTER TEN

HAZEL RAMER WAS sure that over the course of her life she had tried pretty much every neurostimulant that was legal and a good number that weren't. Some of them were better than others and of course you used different things for different reasons. She was particularly fond of a couple of combinations — she liked to be able to feel different emotions and sensations at once. But those she only did online. The implants she and everyone else used to access everywherenet had built in safeguards, so there was no way she could hurt herself with anything she did online, not permanently anyway. And if she was physically safe in her apartment, it didn't really matter if she had a bad reaction. She had her system set to automatically log her off if things got out of control and once she was disconnected, she'd be fine. It had been a long time since it had come to that.

She wasn't one of those poor people you see in doorways and alleys, in those terrible dive bars in the bad parts of the city. She believed that if the chemicals exist to help you feel the way you want to feel, it's just plain stupidity not to take advantage of them. She thought it would be like refusing to talk to people online and only ever meeting face to face. Pointless. These things all existed to make life better, so there was no reason not to use them.

She was thinking about that as she walked home from the train stop. She was remembering her conversation with Dex, his strange refusal to do those little things that made life bearable. He'd always been that way. What was it he said, that he preferred to suffer? She wondered how true that was. He had always had the air of a man with a past, some kind of dark secret, but Hazel always guessed that it was just an act to keep people from trying to get close. He seemed different now, though. Still suffering, but maybe finally learning to enjoy the pain?

Just as those thoughts crossed her mind, she felt a pain of her own. A hand was clapped over her mouth and nose and she felt her left arm being twisted behind her. She tried to scream, but the hand over her face muffled her cries. She felt herself being pulled backward, but she could only limply struggle. She couldn't breathe. She saw a flash of metal under her eyes. There was something in the hand that was over her face, something digging into her cheek. She felt herself begin to panic, when the hand twitched and a jolt of pain shot through her cheek. But as soon as it began, it was over and Hazel felt better.

No, she didn't feel better — Hazel felt great. Where her arm was pinned behind her, the nerves all sang. It was like where there had been pain there was now a pleasurable tingling. Very pleasurable tingling indeed. The hand over her mouth felt like a caress and only its presence stopped her from moaning with pleasure. Even her lungs, starved of air, felt wonderful, like they were snuggled under a warm blanket. Hazel felt herself being stuffed in a box, the cramped quarters cozy as a womb. She felt the box moving — maybe it was a trailer on a scooter, she thought. She never wondered where she was being taken; the trip itself was so wonderful. Every bump and jostle made her muscles tense and contract, the sexual feeling overwhelming.

Finally, the box stopped moving and Hazel saw it open. A man she didn't recognize stood over her, smiling. She smiled back and let him help her out of the box. They were in a small, dirty room, with nothing but a plain metal chair. "Sit," he said, his voice nuzzling her ears. She would do anything for a voice like that, she thought and sat in the chair. She saw him take a length of polymer rope out of one of his pockets and grinned. He was going to tie her up! Just thinking about it made her feel wet between her legs. She couldn't stop herself from uttering small gasps as she let him bind her to the chair.

"Does that feel good?" he asked in that beautiful voice, once she was trussed to the chair. Her arms were pinned behind the chair back, her hands together. She could barely move. The sensation was exquisite.

"Yes," she whispered.

He smiled and took a gleaming knife from a small sheath on his hip. He held it loosely in front of him, at about Hazel's eye level. She was mesmerized by the way the undulating metal of its blade caught the little light in the room. "That's good," he said as he cut away the material of her shirt. Hazel cried out in pleasure as he slipped the knife under the skin of her chest, between her breasts. He was pulling now, tiny drops of blood spattering his face. Hazel had never felt joy like this before.

"That's good," he repeated, his voice like velvet on her skin. "I want to make you feel the way I feel."

CHAPTER ELEVEN

DEX COULDN'T FIND anything about Hazel Ramer. He'd checked B&B's internal board when he'd first gotten in, but there was nothing new. There wasn't even a mention — it was as if nothing had happened. Dex frowned. He knew that B&B's Security would be looking into it; there was the apartment to deal with at a minimum and if she'd had some kind of accident then showed up a few days later to find someone else in her apartment and her job up for grabs, it would be a nightmare of paperwork for her compensation and benefits advisor. Dex guessed that it wouldn't look too good to new hires, either.

But if they were investigating, they were doing it quietly. He connected to the Cubicle Men's system and sent a request to have B&B's Security logs sent to him. The organization had a staff of many people whose talents were more like Annabelle's than Dex's. One of the reasons why the organization encouraged its members to take on low to mid level jobs with the firms was to get access to their internal systems. Over the years, clever crackers had tapped into the Security systems for all of the major firms. It wasn't always on; in order to keep their own access a secret, the organization had to access each system discretely. Dex had the rank and access to get into his own employer's Security files, it just wouldn't be immediate. He figured that he would know whatever the B&B Security people knew by the time he got home.

Or maybe more. Dex guessed that Security would be assuming that Hazel had just taken off, or maybe had some kind of misadventure. He hoped that's all it was, but honestly he doubted it was either. Hazel had never struck Dex as the impulsive type, at least not with her livelihood. And he knew she was smart enough to hit a medclinic if something happened, even if she were high when it did. So long as you're getting your quota of widgets out, corporate couldn't give a shit about what you do. And the firm's medclinic is on retainer, so it's not like they are shelling out any cash to fix up your bangs and bruises. So, Dex figured that there was a good chance that Security was just chasing empty leads. And he had an idea about something he could check that they couldn't.

• • •

It was mid-afternoon, Dex's own personal witching hour. Nothing was worse than an almost but not quite finished work day. He got up from his desk, scowled at Mister Mouse and walked the few metres to the break room. He poured a coffee and thought about Hazel. He liked her, always had, and hoped that she liked him, too. If she was okay and he was just being paranoid, what he was about to do could really piss her off. It seemed like a worthwhile gamble.

Back at his desk, Dex pulled up a client file and started a manual upgrade the client had ordered. While he worked, he used his private access to call Annabelle. "In the afternoon slump, are you?" she asked.

"Am I that predictable?" Dex asked, turning to the wall and subvocalizing so that the prying Mister Mouse didn't have anything to add to the file Dex imagined that he kept on him.

"I'm afraid so," Annabelle said. "So, have you sorted out that thing that was bothering you last night?"

Annabelle kept her voice light, but Dex knew she was concerned. It had doubtlessly taken all her willpower not to call him before he reached out to her. "No," he said simply, "and that's why I called. See, it's not just the two pm blues."

"What's up?" Annabelle asked and Dex told her briefly about Hazel's disappearance. He expected Annabelle to tell him that he was jumping the gun, that a woman he barely knew could be expected to do just about anything and taking off for a few days was not that unusual anyway. He expected her to remind him that the organization's resources were not for his own personal use and that her particular and highly illegal talents weren't his for the taking whenever he felt like it. But she didn't say anything like that. She said, "What can I do to help?" Dex could have kissed her.

"I want to you look for Hazel," he said. "You know, the kind of invasive, immoral cracker way you have." Annabelle had discovered a way to crack into the everywherenet's logs of individual access systems. The public net that everyone used for business, finance, entertainment and more was essentially a public utility run by a cartel of the firms. Almost everyone accessed the system through neural implants which interfaced with personal systems — those internal nodes which held audio and video memories or enhanced cogitation or sensation — and those personal systems were of necessity chock full of identifying information. The everywherenet kept logs of everyone's activities, both online and offline. Hardly anyone ever looked at these files and they were automatically purged within a few days of creation. They existed mostly for cases just like this one, but it took a long time for even a large firm's Security to get access to the information. Hazel had already been gone a couple of days; if Barrett and Brar's Security didn't have the information already, it would probably be gone in a day.

Getting everywherenet's logs for Hazel wasn't the part that Dex worried about and Annabelle agreed readily to check them out. It was his next request that was more of an issue. "So, Annabelle," Dex began, "if you can get into everywherenet's logs, you must be able to trace Hazel once you're in there. You know, tunnel into her own personal system or something, right?"

"Whoa, Dex," Annabelle said. "That's a serious invasion of privacy. I mean, if you'd just decided to say fuck it all or were off on a bender or something, how would you like it to get a knock in your head and have some stranger barge in on your mind? I mean, most people don't even know that that sort of thing can even happen. I can't imagine what that would be like."

"I know it's kind of an extreme idea," Dex said, backpedalling a little. "I just wondered if you could do it; you know, if it seemed like it was the only way."

Annabelle was quiet for a moment and Dex wondered if she was thinking of a way to tell him how appalled she was at him even suggesting such a thing. Privacy was very important to Annabelle, Dex knew, and he was afraid that he'd made a terrible mistake in asking her this. He was trying to figure out a way to get out of this situation when he heard her take a deep breath.

"I can do it," she said carefully, "but just because it's possible does not mean that I should do it."

"Fair enough," Dex said. "It's probably overkill here, anyway. I just feel like my hands are tied, like there's nothing I can do. And while I can't explain it in any way that makes any real sense, I just have a terrible feeling about this. If she's in trouble and I really think she is, if there's any way to help her I want to do it."

"I understand, Dex," Annabelle said and Dex knew that she meant it. "If we find anything more concrete, maybe it is something we could try. Maybe. I'd have to be pretty sure that it was the only way, but I'm not ruling it out completely. I'm just not willing to do it now."

Dex let out a breath he didn't realize he even been holding. "I'm sure that's the right decision," he said. "You'll get the other stuff for me, though?" he asked.

"Of course," Annabelle said, the lightness back in her voice. "I know I have to earn my keep."

Dex laughed. "You earn your keep plenty, kiddo, and it's not by doing anything fancy with cracking into systems, let me tell you."

"You old sweet talker, you," Annabelle said. "Now go back to pretending to work so I can get back to really working. Some of us have things to do in a day, you know," she chided Dex good-naturedly.

"You know, I could help you with that," he answered and ended the call.

• • •

It was less than an hour later, almost the end of his day, when Dex's messenger chirped. It was his boss, Marian, wanting a chat. Dex closed his eyes and sighed. He needed this kind of distraction like a hole in the head. He hadn't spoken with his boss since he'd been put on a kind of employment probation, three-quarters time and pay. It had actually worked out great for him, since he kept his apartment and other benefits and got a shorter workday out of it. But he also knew that it was a last chance kind of thing. One more fuckup and he was out.

He thought about it for a moment. He had no love of his job and B&B. He had some seniority and enjoyed a slightly better apartment for it, but otherwise what he did day in day out would be no different at some other firm. Maybe it was time to move on. Getting canned could actually help him out — they would have to give him severance which he wouldn't get if he quit, so he'd have at least a couple of weeks before he'd have to find another job. Or at least somewhere else to live.

Having decided that he couldn't be bothered to try and keep his job, Dex answered Marian's ping. He heard his boss's voice clearly in his ear and he idly wondered if they gave new management training in how to sound like a dick.

"Andersson," Marian began and Dex sighed inwardly. "I've been looking at your personnel record as part of a periodic review." So this was is, Dex thought. He said nothing and could almost hear Marian's discomfort. He smiled to himself.

"Yes, well," his boss said, unable to bear the silence. "I've been reviewing your file and I've noticed that you have been back on track. No more tardiness, following all the scripts on your calls. Very good, Andersson. I'm pleased to see that you are back on the team." Dex still had nothing to say, but had to make sure his boss knew that he was still there.

"Glad to hear it," he said.

"Unfortunately," Marian's voice became cooler, "we are not yet able to reinstate your full time status." Dex grinned to himself as Marian took on a conspiratorial tone. "I might be able to move forward on that a bit faster if you were to participate in a new program we have instituted. Purely voluntary, of course."

Dex rolled his eyes. "I'm listening," he said.

Marian explained that even with all the monitoring available to them — electronic time stamps, all calls and communications on the system copied and monitored — there were still some things that on the people on the ground could know. "You know," Marian explained, "attitude, team spirit, that sort of thing. We just want you to give us your impressions of your co-workers so we can know you all a bit better."

"You want me to spy on my neighbours?" Dex asked, almost incredulous, but somewhat unsurprised.

"Just if you notice anything that might be relevant," Marian assured him. "It would be a great help to us here and would be duly noted on your record."

Dex contemplated telling his boss what he thought of this scheme, but decided he wasn't quite ready to be fired after all. "I'll see what I can do," he said and ended the call. He sighed and glanced up at Mister Mouse. The other man avoided his gaze and Dex wondered if the other man was in on the scheme or just wanted to be. "You deserve each other," he muttered under his breath, then logged out of his B&B account.

• • •

Dex was already back in his apartment, out of his uniform and into the hideous but comfortable one piece, when Annabelle pinged him. He settled into his comfortable chair and put his feet up on the edge of his table. "So, is this a social call, or do you have news from our great mechanical overlords for me?"

"It's about Hazel," Annabelle said, her voice serious.

Dex's smile slid off his face and he felt the muscles in his neck and shoulders tighten. "What?" he croaked out.

"She's dead," Annabelle said, matter of factly. Dex felt the air leave his lungs like he was being deflated.

"You're sure?" he asked, knowing that Annabelle would never have told him something like that without being one hundred percent sure.

"I'm sure," she said, her voice soft. "Remember I told you how if someone is logged into the 'nets when they die, there's this specific data pattern that shows up on the logs?" Dex nodded, which Annabelle wouldn't have known since they were using a voice only connection, but she continued anyway. "Well, there's a very clear instance of it for her. For two nights ago. At 03:07 UTC. I make that early evening your time."

"Jesus, Annabelle," Dex said. "Somehow I thought it was too late, but I still hoped, you know? That she was just on a bad stim trip or, I don't know, lying in a ditch with a headache and no memory or something. Goddamn it!" he exploded and slammed his fist into the arm of his chair. He said nothing for a moment and Annabelle didn't interrupt his silence. "Any idea what happened?"

"Not yet," Annabelle said, "but I'm trying to track her identity chip and see if I can figure out where she is."

"You mean, where her body is," Dex said bitterly.

"Yes," Annabelle said quietly. They were both quiet for a while.

"I'm sorry," Dex said, "I didn't mean to take it out on you."

"You didn't," Annabelle said. "And I'm the one who's sorry. She was your friend — this must be very hard."

"She wasn't my friend," Dex said sadly. "We sat next to each other at work for a couple of years and complained about the coffee everyday. I didn't even know she used stims until the other day. I don't know where she lives, or even who to notify about this. She was just another person I barely noticed on the edge of my life. And now she's gone and that's all she'll ever be."

Chapter Twelve

Annabelle and Dex talked for another hour, mostly Annabelle listening to Dex alternately rage about Hazel's death and moan about he'd hardly even gotten to know her. Annabelle said little, other than to remind Dex that what happened to Hazel could not possibly be his fault. She promised that she would do what she could to track Hazel's movements in the hours before she died, following the signals in the chip embedded in Hazel's hand. Identity chips didn't broadcast unless they were in use, so you couldn't really track a person using them. However, Annabelle had found that a careful reading of their logs often painted a picture which could be used to recreate a particular period of time for a person. She was quite good at it and it was one of the reasons why she was so well regarded among the Cubicle Men.

After Annabelle extracted a promise from Dex that he would not go and do anything until the next day, she rang off to begin her search. Dex was torn. One part of him wanted to break his word and hit the streets, trying to find Hazel's body by breaking down every door in the city. The other part of him wanted to forget that Hazel was gone, forget that he would be unable to let this go. It wasn't his case, would probably never be his case even if someone did come to the organization looking for a resolution. But he was stuck with it, he knew. He would never be able to just let it go. But maybe for a few hours on this night, he could forget.

He walked to the cupboard and pulled down the bottle of Jamaica's Best. He poured a tumbler half full of the dark brown liquor and tossed it back, downing the drink in one swallow. He grimaced and refilled his glass, then pulled a bottle of gingapop from the cooler. He splashed the soda into the glass, diluting the drink slightly. He took a sip and walked back to the chair with the drink in his hand.

He needed something to distract him, or he would spend the whole night trying to solve the case without any information. The rum was starting to burn his belly and he felt the warmth spread through his body. The familiar feeling made his thoughts start to mellow and he found himself accessing his video library. He recorded his life as a matter of course, but other than experiences relating to cases, he only kept the interesting parts. There were a great many of those, though, mostly from his youth as a musician. He picked one of those, a particularly smoking night in a terrible bar in the part of town where unemployed people tended to live.

The bar was barely a functional room, its thin walls bleeding the sound of its bands out to the street where there were always people trying to sleep. The stage was nothing more than a small rise built of junk that the bar's owners had found in the alleys behind the building. Dex always worried that the stage was going to break under the weight of himself and his three bandmates. The drinks were watered down and food was nonexistent. But Milo's New City Lounge consistently had the best audience of any of the venues Dex played. It had been his favourite place in the world.

The video Dex chose was from one of the first gigs he'd played at Milo's and before he even started the file playing, he remembered the combination of nerves, booze, and excitement. He started the video just before they had gone on stage and watched himself sitting in a chair at a table offstage that Milo's provided for the musicians. He saw himself drain the last of his beer and slap the glass on the table across from Jennie, the mixer and synth player. "Let's get it on," he heard her say, as he saw her stand. The view shifted as he had stood himself, the recording taken from his own perspective. It wasn't exactly like being there, but the combination of memory and the video made watching the events almost seem like it was happening to him all over again.

He walked behind Jennie, Maksym pulling up the rear, as they climbed on to the rickety stage. Jennie's small deck and keyboards were already set up, while Dex carried his mandolin and Maks had his guitar slung over his back on a strap. The crowd roared into life as they made their way to their places, the ovation huge even though Dex was sure that hardly anyone in the place had heard them play before. He remembered that the three of them had been playing weekly at their regular watering hole, J.T.'s and that they'd been invited to play a cancellation slot at Milo's when the owner had stopped in one Thursday. They didn't even have a name for the group.

Dex watched as he, Maks and Jennie played to the smoky room, the video a little dark and grainy. It must have been before he'd gotten the upgrade which compensated for poor lighting. Even so, the audio was crystal clear and by the time they were into the third song, he wasn't even really watching any more. He was letting the music wash over him, the riffs of his mandolin merging with the twangs from Maks's guitar, with the strange sonic waves that Jennie created sweeping over both of their instruments. Dex found himself fingering the arms of his chair as he listened, between long, slow sips of his drink.

At the back of his mind, Dex knew that he was in for an unpleasant morning if he kept this up, but at that moment he just didn't care. He wanted the memories, the release from his present. He didn't want to think about his job at B&B, about Hazel or even about Annabelle. He wanted to be lost in his past, back in a place where he maybe didn't have a lot of security but he never felt out of place. With the video still running before his vision, he picked up the mandolin Annabelle had given him when he was visiting her. It was nothing like the one he watching himself play in the video — that one had been an antique, made of real wood. He'd sold it when Maks left; he wasn't going to play it alone and it was just a reminder of a life he was trying to leave behind him. At least that was what he'd thought at the time. Later he regretted losing the instrument almost as much as he regretted everything else.

He had told Annabelle about his old days as a musician, but he thought he'd always made it clear that those days were in his past, that he didn't miss playing. But when he was in Nice visiting her, she pulled out a large parcel on the day before he was going to leave. She had made a particular effort that night, Dex remembered. She had sprung for a take out meal made from real ingredients, not the ubiquitous nutrient blocks that Dex, like most people, lived off. The dinner was strange to Dex, who was unaccustomed to even vat grown or synthesized food. He didn't think Annabelle cared for it much either, but he knew it was the thought that mattered. She was trying — trying to be with him in an embodied, physical way, even though she recoiled from the physical world as much as Dex did from the virtual one.

After the bizarre dinner, she sat near Dex on the small sofa in her apartment. Her place wasn't really that much bigger than the one Dex lived in, but it was worlds away in terms of its appointments. She had a separate bedroom and the main room had a couch as well as a table and chairs. The furniture looked like it actually had been designed for human beings and Annabelle told Dex that she'd been allowed to choose her own things from a catalogue her personnel manager gave her when she started her job. "So that's what it's like at the top," Dex had said, smiling.

"I'm not at the top of anything," Annabelle had answered, chiding Dex but laughing. "I'm just a working stiff just like you, they only pay me more."

"Well, you're tops in my books," Dex had said, waggling his eyebrows. Annabelle had rolled her eyes, but Dex could see that a slight flush had appeared at the edges of her cheek. He'd begun to recognize that this was a sign that she was flattered. He'd begun to really like seeing it. He wanted to reach out and touch her, but he knew from experience that it would ruin the mood. She would flinch and shrink from his hand, or worse, try to pretend that everything was fine while she suffered. He had stopped trying, hoping that one day she would come to him. He was starting to think that it would never happen and he tried to imagine a way for him to be happy without it, without her touch. He wasn't sure it would ever work, but at times like these he was willing to try.

She had shuffled a little on the couch and looked at him shyly though lowered eyelids. He often wondered how someone who so clearly disdained the physical world could be so good at communicating without words. "What?" he'd asked, unable to keep a curious grin from his face. "What are you up to?"

"I've got a surprise for you," she had said and for a brief moment Dex's heart flipped and he thought she was going to touch him. But instead, she reached behind the couch and retrieved a large box, wrapped in some kind of thin film. She handed it to Dex and he raised an eyebrow. "Just open it," she said, smiling shyly. "I hope you like it."

When he first saw the mandolin in the box, Dex was shocked. He never thought he would play again; it had never even occurred to him to try. Music for him was locked in the past. But he couldn't help but pluck one of its strings and the sound resonated in his chest like a thousand memories. Annabelle was looking at him, expectation and concern clear in her eyes. "Is it okay?" she asked, nervous all of a sudden.

Dex's mind was churning, trying desperately to come up with strategies to hide from Annabelle what a terrible mistake the gift had been when he realized that he wasn't feeling the overwhelming sadness he associated with things that reminded him of those days. Amazed, he looked into her eyes and said, honestly, "Yes. It is okay. Thank you."

He had played the mandolin a few times since he'd returned to the city, but never like this. He played along with the video memory, the notes coming back slowly but steadily as he moved from song to song. He stopped every couple of songs to refill his glass and as the level in the bottle dropped he began playing with more feeling, more freedom. He played through the whole video, the full three hours that he'd played in Milo's so many years before. After the video was done, he played on his own until he could barely see the strings, let alone carry a tune. He left his glass on the arm of the chair and fell into the bed, still wearing his ugly one piece.

CHAPTER THIRTEEN

THE MORNING DAWNED grey and early. The slight trickle of light which shone through Dex's small window cut a laser through his head and he barely made it to the lav before his stomach rebelled. After a few minutes of heaving, he stripped out of the stained one piece and turned on the shower. Once the water was gone and he was dry, he made his way back to the bed and the bottle of Flying Fish. He took a large swig and through sheer force of will kept it down. In a minute he was feeling better. Not well, not even truly human, but better.

He opened the autoclave and swapped his clean uniform for the nasty one piece. He dressed, stuffed a couple of food bricks in his pocket and walked out of the apartment. He stopped briefly at a kiosk for a decent cup of strong coffee before catching the train to work.

At his desk he avoided Mister Mouse's accusing eyes and checked the internal boards. He was becoming quite the model employee on that front. He knew that the managers knew who read what and wondered if this would counteract some of the black marks he knew were next to his name on some personnel file somewhere. He didn't care one way or another. If they fired him he'd be so much happier, at least until his two week severance period ended and he got kicked out of his apartment.

Again, there was nothing about Hazel. He wondered if B&B's Security even knew she was dead yet. He hadn't even bothered to log into the Cubicle Men's system after Annabelle gave him the news. He couldn't imagine what Security could have learned that would help him and he'd just wanted to forget. Now, though, with a still slightly pounding head and a roiling stomach, he knew he would have to go through the Security files carefully. The initial shock of Hazel's death was past, now, and Dex had moved on to that obsessive state which made him such a good detective.

While he answered a customer enquiry about warranty replacements for parts which had been incorrectly installed, he fired up his back door access out of Barrett and Brar's internal system. He logged into his account with the Cubicle Men and saw that he had three messages. The first was a notification from his clients on the housing case. They were unanimously unhappy that their employers were going to get away with providing such substandard living quarters, but they realized that they had no binding way to force the firm into anything. They were willing to fix the things they could and asked Dex to set it up. He forwarded their message directly to Pat Malone, with a short covering note asking the other man to do what he needed to in order to have his connection with the printer to help them.

His next message was from the automated system, with a link to the live tunnel into the B&B Security system. Dex would have access to anything they were doing, including internal memos and messages. He wouldn't be able to change anything, but he could look. He saw that the access was good only for 48 hours and most of that time had passed already. Because of the time crunch, ordinarily he would have just ignored the other message in the queue, but it was from Captain Zhang and it was specifically to Dex.

"I saw your request for access to Barrett and Brar's Security logs," she wrote. "I know you aren't assigned to any cases that have anything to do with them and I also know that they are your employer. I've let the access come though, because you've never fucked around before and it might be urgent. But I want to know what you're up to. You've got two days access for free, but that's the end of it until you get me up to speed. Also, good work on the housing case. I knew you'd figure a way out with sufficient motivation. —ZZ."

Dex didn't begrudge the captain her concern. There was nothing inherently wrong with investigating a case related to your own employer, but it was unusual. Most cases came though a central clearinghouse and were assigned by the captain or one of her lieutenants. Generally, detectives would never get assigned a case which had anything to do with their own employers. Some clients, though, sought out individual detectives or were referred to a particular person. Usually, those cases stayed with the D who brought them in, even if there was a conflict of interest. The organization had found over the years that when people came to a particular individual for help, they felt most comfortable dealing only with that person. And while the organization encouraged its members to have regular jobs, it also expected that those jobs would be relatively transitory. The nature of their clandestine work dictated that their people would be fired on occasion or at least have to move on voluntarily from time to time in order to keep their work for the organization a secret.

Dex would explain what was going on to the captain later, though. He was running out of time to see what B&B's Security had discovered and while he didn't expect there to be any great revelations, he couldn't afford to be wrong and miss something. He linked into the cracked opening to B&B's Security system, noting that he had less than 24 hours of access left. He wasn't sure how much junk he would have to go through to find what he needed and if they were actively pursuing leads, he would want to follow their live conversations.

The system was typical of most corporate Security teams Dex

had seen. It wasn't all that dissimilar to the Cubicle Men's system — there was a messaging client, assignment centre and file storage. Each case had a directory with reports and information which was accessible based on rank and profile, so that the higher ups could see everything that was going on, but lower level staff had more restricted access. Dex, of course, had access to everything.

They had done all the usual things — checked all of Hazel's incoming and outgoing text and voice messages from work, but they'd found nothing strange there. After she didn't turn up for work for a day, a couple of the bruisers went out to her apartment and poked around. There was a video file of the search and Dex watched as these monkeys pawed through her things like common burglars. From the video file Dex could see that Hazel's apartment was a little larger and nicer than his but not in the same league as Annabelle's. He was surprised; he would have thought that a sales job would come with much better digs than his lowly CSR apartment.

Hazel lived alone and it looked like she wasn't into a lot of physical world activities. Her small closet held her B&B uniforms, a few casual outfits and that was about it. In the rest of her apartment, Dex could see no decoration, toys, tools or supplies. It was an entirely normal apartment and it looked very much like it should have if she'd just left for work one morning and never come back. There was even a dirty coffee cup on the small counter next to the autoclave. Dex was even more sure that whatever happened to her, she had planned to be back that day.

He started paging around the reports and discussion of B&B's Security. There wasn't much activity; he could see that it wasn't a high priority item for them. There was only one officer assigned to the case, a class 4 named Monika Raff and she had a half dozen other items on her docket. It looked like she was half heartedly trying to find friends or family to notify or interrogate. She'd sent a request to everyone in Hazel's private contact list, but there were only a handful of names. Looking at Raff's private messenger, Dex saw that she'd received two responses to her queries and hadn't even looked at them yet. He couldn't really fault the officer — missing persons wasn't exactly something they dealt with every day and the sad truth was that the bosses at B&B didn't really care much about the fate of one employee. They were probably more concerned about finalizing the state of Hazel's clients and apartment than what actually happened to her.

Dex spent a few more minutes poking around the Security files, but there wasn't anything else there. He took the contact information for Monika Raff, in case he wanted to talk to her, but he didn't think they would find anything new before he did. He logged out of his tunnel into the B&B Security system, after copying everything to his own disk first. He would open a case on the Cubicle Men's system and dump all the B&B's information into that file for reference. As far as he could tell, only he and Annabelle knew that Hazel was dead, which meant that all the access in the world to the B&B Security files wasn't going to do much for him. His own investigation was the best bet for finding out what happened and he didn't even have anywhere to begin.

CHAPTER FOURTEEN

WHEN DEX GOT back to his apartment, he changed and ate, then sat in his comfortable chair, unfocussed from his apartment and logged into the Cubicle Men's system. He quickly updated Captain Zhang on Hazel's disappearance. He didn't mention her death, not yet. He knew the captain extended him a fair amount of latitude, but he didn't want to let on that he was using Annabelle's skills before there was a real case file started. He didn't want the captain to think that he was abusing his relationship with Annabelle, even though he thought that was exactly what he was doing. Annabelle had made her interest in Dex clear long ago and had always been more than willing to give him whatever he wanted in the way of help, or anything else. But now that their relationship had changed, Dex felt awkward taking Annabelle's help on cases that weren't officially on the books. Or, more accurately, he felt awkward having the captain know about it.

So, once his message was sent, he set about legitimizing his investigation by making a case file. It was tedious work, but Dex found that organizing his thoughts into a written report often helped him find things he'd overlooked in a case. He liked the way it forced his haphazard ideas into a linear format and gave him a better sense of the situation. He copied the information he'd taken from B&B's system into the case file and wrote up a summary of his investigation. He was finishing up this preliminary report, trying to figure out when to add the information Annabelle had given him about Hazel's death so it looked like he'd enlisted her help after the case was properly opened, when his system pinged. He saved his work and saw that it was Annabelle calling. He realized that it was the first time in weeks that he hadn't heard from her or called her himself by this time of day. He wondered briefly if everything was okay.

"Hi," he said. "I'm just getting a case file open for this thing with Hazel," Dex said. "How has your day been?"

"I've had better ones," Annabelle said and Dex thought her voice sounded tired. "Work was tough; I'm having to cover for someone so that means a bunch of extra tasks. Not a real problem, just a pain in the ass, you know?"

"Sure," Dex said, feeling bad about always asking her to drop everything and help him whenever he needed some sneaky systems work. He knew that her day job was not only more demanding than his, but was work she actually enjoyed. Sometimes he forgot that not everyone held his cavalier attitude toward continued employment. "You should take the night off, maybe," he said. "Watch a vid or go out for a drink or something."

"Are you asking me on a date?" Annabelle said, the usual twinkle in her voice returning briefly.

"Uh," Dex stalled, "I was thinking I'd be busy tonight on getting this case organized." He heard Annabelle sigh. He quickly scanned his report and saw that he didn't have much left that he could add and without any new information he didn't really have anywhere to go on the investigation. "On the other hand," he said, "I could maybe stand a break, too." Dex swore he could hear Annabelle's smile.

"See you in Monte's in half an hour?" she suggested.

"Sure," Dex said.

• • •

Dex linked into the bar and recognized a few other Cubicle Men detectives at the small tables. Most were alone or with one other person and none of them seemed to pay much attention to Dex's arrival. That was one of the things he liked about Monte's — everyone kept pretty much to themselves. It wasn't the same as being in a real pub, but even before he started keeping time with Annabelle, Dex would spend a few nights a week there. Like everyone, he needed a better view than the four walls of his apartment every once and again.

He didn't see Annabelle waiting at any of the tables, so he ambled over to one of his usual booths along the far wall. Through the heads up interface he ordered his usual: a non-stim dark and stormy and a pack of virtual cigarettes. The drink materialized in front of his right hand, sweating slightly over a deep cherry red napkin. The smokes appeared just in front of the glass, a silver lighter on top of the red and gold pack. He took a sip of the drink, the simulated taste of it sharp on his dry tongue. He shook a cigarette out of the pack, lit it and sucked a plume of smoke into his rendered lungs. He didn't taste anything; the cigarettes were all for show, like a necklace or fancy hairdo. It had been donkey's years since he had put anything on fire into his mouth in the physical world, but he admitted that he liked the way his avatar looked like with a smoke, so it was one of his few concessions to the virtual world.

He was stubbing out the cigarette when Annabelle materialized just inside the bar's door. Dex was relieved to see that she hadn't dressed up or anything. Her avatar wore her usual slim brown trousers and artsy printed tee shirt. Dex stood as he waited for her to approach the table. However, he watched as she recognized someone at the bar and walked over to him. He was rooted to the spot as he watched her greet the tall, very muscular broad-shouldered man warmly, briefly hugging him and letting him kiss her cheek.

Dex found his feet and slipped out of the banquette. Surprised by the pang of jealousy he felt as he watched her giggle at something the man said, Dex forced himself to walk over to the couple, sure to keep his avatar's face neutral. Annabelle saw him before he could say anything and smiled. She turned her companion to face Dex as well and said, "Dex! What a coincidence. You should meet Neil Weisman. Sarge, this is my good friend, Andersson Dexter."

Dex faced the other man and had to look up. Weisman's avatar was enormous. He looked like he had muscles on his muscles, the bulges rippling under a tight button down shirt. He grinned widely at Dex, though, and stuck out a massive paw. "Mr. Dexter," he said, his voice gravel. "Good to meet you." They shook hands and Dex looked past the giant at Annabelle, who smiled happily.

"Nice to meet you," he said, withdrawing his hand. "And how do you two know each other?" he asked, oddly afraid of the answer.

"Out there," Weisman answered bluntly and Dex nearly fell over.

His equilibrium was not improved when Annabelle added, "Sarge and I are old army buddies."

• • •

"You were in the army?" Dex repeated, after the three of them had gone back to Dex's booth and were seated with drinks.

"It wasn't for long," Annabelle said.

"She wasn't exactly cut out for it," the giant man added.

"I'd think not," Dex said, looking at Annabelle out of the corner of his eye. "I don't know a lot about the military," he continued, "but I'm pretty sure it's all running and jumping and it's all out there, right?"

Annabelle laughed. "Yup," she said. "The running and jumping wasn't that much of a problem. I didn't mind that stuff too much. It was all the hand to hand combat that did me in."

"Actually, she was pretty good at that, too," Weisman said, smiling. "She could even drop me most of the time."

"I just hated every second of it," she said, scowling. "I had a real incentive to end the fight fast."

"So, whatever compelled you to enlist in the army?" Dex asked, still incredulous.

"I was still trying to make myself become normal," she said. Dex glanced at Weisman and Annabelle caught the look. "It's okay," she said. "Sarge knows as much about me as anyone. He was one of the leaders of my unit back then and helped me get out of my contract early." She looked over at the big man with a warm smile. "He understood."

Dex's eyebrows lifted, but he didn't want to pry.

"I'm not all that different from Lewis, here," Weisman volunteered. "I lost my legs in an ordnance accident twenty ago, so I wear these fancy prostheses out there. I can outrun slow vehicles now, jump over twenty metres. It's great for an infantryman like me. But all the time I'm out there, I miss this," he stood and slapped his thigh. "So, I spend all my free time in M City. It's where I feel like a real person." He caught Annabelle's eyes and they shared a smile.

Dex shook his head. "Just when I think I've got you sussed, you find some new way to surprise me," he said to Annabelle.

"A girl's got to have a little mystery," Annabelle said, grinning.

• • •

They finished their drinks, then Weisman excused himself and linked out of the bar. Annabelle scooted over to sit next to Dex and they briefly embraced, Dex kissing her cheek. He had gotten so used to this action by now that it barely bothered him any more. Another shimmering green drink appeared before her and Dex knew that it would be a stim-laced cocktail of some sort. He watched her take a sip and saw a flush of warmth cross her cheeks. He wondered what real-world sensation that image was simulating.

"What a great idea this was," Annabelle said, putting her drink down in front of her. "I haven't seen Sarge in years and I'm already feeling a million times better. You were right, I needed this."

"Yeah," Dex said, "you sounded like you were getting a little wound up." Annabelle stretched and ran her hands thorough her hair.

"It's just work," she said. "I like it, so it's never that bad. Right now things are very 'time sensitive', as the management drones would say. I don't have a problem with real deadlines or urgencies, but I can't help but get annoyed when it's somehow my problem that someone else didn't turn up and finish their tasks." She sighed and took another sip of her drink.

"That's life in the big city, kiddo," Dex said, smiling.

"I know," Annabelle said. "I'm not trying to make it sound like my problems are unique, they just piss me off, that's all."

"Understandable," Dex said. "The one joy of having a shitty job is that no one really expects anything of you."

"Maybe that's the way it is with your employer," Annabelle said, "but we all know your real work is with the organization and you take that plenty seriously indeed."

"Sure," Dex conceded, "but Zizou doesn't treat us like children. I get more respect from her than I do from my bosses at B&B by a lightyear."

"It's different, Dex," Annabelle said. "You know it is." He just nodded and they sat in silence for a moment, the virtual smoke from Dex's cigarette spiraling in almost random patterns between them. "Speaking of real work," Annabelle broke the silence, "I wrote a script to look for Hazel's ID chip trail. I've been getting bits and pieces over the last 24 hours, but it's going to take a bit more time to compile it all."

"Jesus, Annabelle," Dex said. "You don't have to do that right now. I mean, if you're swamped at work you shouldn't be spending time on this stuff for me. Shit, I haven't even put the information you've already given me in my report for Zizou, yet."

"Come on, Dex," Annabelle said, smiling wryly. "I like my job plenty, but you can't expect me to believe that you think that writing code to make the trains run on time is in the same league as helping to solve a possible murder."

Dex blinked at her and let a beat pass. "Murder," he echoed, finally.

"Well," Annabelle said, looking away, "it's a possibility we have to consider, particularly since her body hasn't been found yet."

"How do you know it hasn't?" Dex asked, more sharply than he'd intended.

"You aren't the only one who reads the daily reports, you know," Annabelle said. "The only reported body in the last week was that one Malone was talking about at the meeting and that was before Hazel disappeared, right?"

"Yeah," Dex said. "And it was male."

"Doesn't necessarily mean anything," Annabelle said quietly.

"True enough," Dex said, "but I saw the image and it wasn't her. So, yeah, it looks like she hasn't turned up yet."

"Hopefully I'll have something for you tomorrow," Annabelle said. "If not, I'll get something to you the next day for sure. I'm on weekend after tomorrow and this is my first priority."

"You're the best, kiddo," Dex said, smiling. "You're way too good to me."

"Just as I keep telling you," Annabelle said, laughing. "But really, people don't just disappear and die. And with your friend Hazel now and that other body last week, it seems like this is maybe a big deal."

Dex's head snapped up to look at Annabelle. "What did you just say?"

Annabelle frowned, puzzled. "I said that this might be a big deal..."

"No," Dex said, "the other body. There might be a connection. I hadn't even thought of that." He stood and leaned across the table, kissing Annabelle. "Thank you. I have to look into that right now. I'll talk to you tomorrow." He winked out of the bar right before Annabelle's eyes.

She blinked a few times in surprise, then sat back in her chair and laughed to herself. "That's my man," she said softly to no one and sipped her drink.

CHAPTER FIFTEEN

DEX REFOCUSSED ON his apartment with a slight twinge of nausea. He stood and went to the cupboard where he grabbed a glass which he filled with water. Working the kinks out of his neck, he sat back down and logged into the Cubicle Men's system again. He ran a search for anything new on the body Pat Malone's team had found the previous week.

There was a lot of information. They'd identified the man as Luis Harker, a tech at a mid level upgrade salon. He was young, only 46 years old, and in life had had the fashionable body often seen on front end workers in salons. His skin was dark and he was softer in the middle than most people. Under the softness, though was the lean hard muscle created by the nutrition cocktail in the mass produced food supply. He was, in essence, a typical young man. He didn't look particularly typical in the images on file, though. The skin on his chest had been cut off in long strips, the edges clean and straight. It was hard to tell in the images, but the written report indicated that there were six separate strips cut from his chest and two from his left thigh. His right thigh had one strip that was still hanging on, as if the cutter had stopped in mid-slice.

Dex looked at the images of the corpse, taken when the body was found on the floor of the squalid room. There were close up shots of the wounds, which Dex skipped over quickly, spending more time on the images of the man's wrists and arms. There were clearly visible lines ringing the wrists and similar fainter ones along the outside of his upper arms. He magnified the images and stared at the marks. The ones on the arms were not uniform and it looked like maybe there were two or three marks on each arm. The ones around the wrists seemed different, thicker perhaps and more pronounced. Dex didn't want to jump to conclusions, but the bruises made it look very much as if the man had been restrained somehow.

Dex then looked at the images of the man's face. His face was unmarked, a classically handsome profile that, like his body, was attractive in a nondescript kind of way. The eyes were mercifully closed — Dex had seen more dead bodies than he ever wanted to during his tour on the goon squad and it was the sightless eyes which had always gotten to him. Dead, staring things, all the fire gone from them. He'd be happy never to see those again. He scrutinized the image, looking for any sign on the man's face as to what happened to him. It was disconcerting — there was no doubt that the man looked happy. Dex was certain the that shape of the lips wasn't a rictus of fear or pain, it was a smile. Luis Harker had gone smiling to his death.

Dex shook his head and hid the images. He pulled up the written report and started wading through it. He scanned it for odd bits of information which jumped out at him, like the location where the body was found and the fact that fibres of polymer rope were found near the corpse. There were also indications in the dirt on the floor of scuff marks that didn't seem to match where the body was lying or look like footprints. Dex guessed that it looked like some kind of item had been removed from the scene. There was plenty of blood on the body and the floor of the room, but the skin from the man's torso and leg was nowhere to be found and there was no sign of a laser cutter or blade. Whether it was murder or something else, one way or another there had to be another person involved.

Dex refocussed on his apartment and took a breath. There was no reason to think that this body was related to Hazel's death — he didn't even know where her body was, let alone what had happened to her. He had to wonder about the timing, though. There wasn't a lot of violent crime in the city. Sure, there were bad areas of town, green and brown sectors could be rough, there was no doubt. But most of the problems were personal disputes and while there were plenty of fights, they rarely ended in death. Even when they did, it was a broken neck or a laser burn, not blood loss from flaying. This was definitely something Dex had never seen before, not on the streets or as a detective and it worried him.

He couldn't help it, but he wondered if a similar fate had befallen Hazel. He imagined her bound, some crazy with a cutter letting loose on her body. He wondered about the look on the other victim, Harker's, face. How could someone be happy while that was going on? Or was it really a look of relief, some kind of joy that the torment was finally over? Dex felt sick. He took a drink of water and stood. He paced around his small apartment until the feeling passed.

He wished Annabelle had found something already, but he knew he couldn't push her. She would be generous with her time, he knew, and would never tell him that he was asking too much, but it wasn't fair to her to keep expecting her to drop everything and work on his projects. For all he knew, she was still busy with her own case — the intellectual property thing. He hadn't even asked her about it.

Dex felt like a heel. It was typical — he was so absorbed in his own work that he forgot that anyone else had anything important going on. That never used to be an issue, when he kept to himself and only ever dealt with other people on a professional level. Now, though, it was different. He wondered, not for the first time, what Annabelle saw in him. He sighed and wished he didn't have to go in to Barrett and Brar the next morning, but he was still two days out from his weekend.

This was not a new feeling. In fact, Dex regularly wished that he didn't have his day job. He doubted that it was unique; he heard plenty of griping in the break room at B&B as well as among the other detectives on the squad. Most of the other Ds worked at jobs not unlike Dex's — well below their abilities. Even Annabelle had been working at a much simpler and less interesting position for years, but her bosses couldn't help but notice her abilities and, surprisingly, they promoted her.

Dex knew she hadn't mentioned the promotion to Zahara Zhang, since the Cubicle Men had a policy which expected its member to have jobs, but nothing too strenuous. The organization paid well, so the poor remuneration wasn't an issue and they also expected its members to be surreptitiously making use of their employers' resources. They existed to fill a gap that was created by the firms' complete control over every aspect of most people's lives and their refusal to do anything for their employees that didn't effect their profit margins. On the face of it The Cubicle Men were just a bunch of loosely organized vigilantes, or a glorified private detective agency, but in many ways they were more political than they appeared.

Annabelle wasn't in it to stick it to the firms, though. Dex knew she had no particular love of her employer or the status quo, but she did love her work. She loved poking around inside systems and she didn't really care whether it was authorized or not. Dex didn't know how she managed to do it, but even after she was promoted and her day job became much more involved, she still managed to be active in the organization, not just with her own cases, but helping the detectives. Dex knew he wasn't the only one who begged her help for anything technical. She was a very popular person in the squad.

She was a great person, a great woman. Dex never understood what it was about him that drew her to him. He had rebuffed her advances for years, for all the same reasons they both struggled with now that they were together. He had often made it clear to her that he knew they were simply incompatible, but she still wouldn't give up on him. She was brilliant, talented and beautiful and he was just an old man who was born too late. He hated himself for keeping her from being happy, but now that he'd embarked on this crazy relationship with her, he wasn't willing to let her go. Not when he'd finally managed to carve a sliver of happiness out of this world that he was convinced he couldn't understand and it was all because of her. And he took her for granted.

If ever there was a night that cried out for getting lost in the bottle of Jamaica's Best, this was it. But that was one of the other things Annabelle had taught him, by her example not by hectoring — she never complained about his habits, never scolded or nagged. She simply managed her social life, her regular work and her cases for the organization. She got it done, whatever it took, because she had responsibilities. Dex had responsibilities, too — not his job, not B&B, but to himself and to his cases. He knew that he cared more about that than he did about drowning his sorrows, so he undressed, took a hit of SleepingJuice and went to bed.

Chapter Sixteen

THE MAN SAT alone, in the dark, in the small apartment. Gerry had gone out somewhere, the man didn't know where. It didn't matter. He sat on his narrow bed, legs crossed, leaning into the wall. There was a small window high on the wall above from him and he could see the lights of the city reflected on the walls. He kept the apartment's lights off. He had taken out the box of tools he kept in the carrier on his scooter. He opened it and pulled something out. It was long and thin and looked like a bit of food brick left out in the sun. He had dried it out in the zapper on another night when Gerry had been out and added it to his collection. This one had been from an earlier candidate, one that had gone well.

The last one had been different. It was the new 'buzzer, of course. Her reactions had been so intense, so powerful, it had thrown him off. He hadn't expected it, but he should have known. He hadn't had enough time alone to try the 'buzzer on himself — he wasn't willing to get off when Gerry was there and this was the first time he had been alone in the apartment for days. He knew that the reaction would be stronger, but how much stronger had been a surprise. He didn't like surprises.

He wasn't sure that he liked the powerful pleasure she seemed to get from the jolt. He knew the 'buzzer was configurable, but that would be a trial and error procedure. And, of course, each person's response was different, so he could never be absolutely sure what it would be like with someone new. It was the same with his old unit, of course, but its highest setting had never been as strong as just the default was on the new one. He was beginning to regret having traded his old unit in.

It had been distracting and once he began the work with the knife, her moans were so loud he worried that they might be discovered. They hadn't been disturbed, though, and he could always add a gag to the procedure, so there was no problem there. It wasn't that he begrudged her the pleasure, or even that it was distracting. The trouble was that it just didn't feel right. It was supposed to be his decision what she felt, his decision whether she was a candidate or not, his choice how, when and if she died. But the new 'buzzer took some of that control away and he didn't like it; he didn't like it at all.

• • •

He had no interest in hurting the candidates, that was why he used the 'buzzer in the first place. When he'd started the work, he had chosen people who were already high on physical stims. He'd moved on to the 'buzzers after only two candidates, though. He didn't like meeting the people in the physical world, didn't like them looking at him while he determined if they were acceptable. The first candidate had been fine, happily flying in his own personal world of mental joy while the man did the work. The second one, though, had been much less successful. He didn't like thinking about that particular candidate, but the thought came unbidden to his mind.

It had been raining slightly and when they left the stim joint the candidate seemed to be high and fine. She tilted her face up toward the falling water, her eyes closed as the drops hit her face. The man grabbed her then, slipping the crook of his arm under her chin. He squeezed, just enough for her body to become pliable, then he put her in the cargo carrier attached to the back of his scooter.

She was quiet as he drove to the spot he'd found, driving right in to the derelict building and into the small room he'd prepared. He hauled her out of the box and wrestled her into the chair. He was excited. He remembered the sense of completion he'd felt with the first candidate when the cutting started, the feeling of calm and control when the man had died. He wanted those feelings again, wanted them so much his hands were shaking.

He tied her hands behind the chair back and bound her body to the chair. He didn't know how much she would struggle and he wanted to have his hands free for the work. She was starting to wake up as he finished the last knot and he waited for her to open her eyes. Her eyelids fluttered and he smiled as he waited for her to become alert. "Where..." she croaked out, as her eyes adjusted to the dim room. "Where am I?"

"Don't worry about that," he said, keeping his voice calm and soothing, waiting for the stims to kick back in. "Everything is just fine." But it wasn't fine. She began to thrash in the chair, trying to loosen the bindings around her. Once she found her voice, she started screaming and he began to panic. The building they were in was abandoned, but that didn't mean it was necessarily ignored. And even though screams and shouts were not uncommon in this neighbourhood, he couldn't be sure that some curious streeter wouldn't be attracted by the noise. She had seemed so happy, so blissed out at the stim joint — he couldn't understand what was happening here. But there was nothing he could do to shut her up other than hit her until she was quiet, so that was what he did.

He never knew if it was the blows of his fist or the blade of his knife which finally finished her. He was so distraught by the end that he swore that this would be the last one; he was finished with the work. It had taken him weeks to realize that he couldn't be finished, that the work was his life. And he found another way to be sure to keep them quiet, keep them compliant and happy. As it turned out, the 'buzzers were much better than physical stims. Even now he admitted that this last one was a million times better than the thrasher had been.

But for the first time since then, the man didn't have the wonderful calm feeling after the work was done. Now he felt twitchy and strange, like he'd taken part in some ritual that he didn't fully understand, like someone else was in control. And that was unacceptable. He needed to find a way to control the candidates, control himself again. He caught himself glancing at the apartment door, as if it could tell him when Gerry would return.

He pulled the new 'buzzer from its place in his tool box, next to the knife and opened the small settings hatch. He turned it down to the lowest setting. He would have to systematically try them all until he found one that was right, one that was appropriate. He went into the lav, locked the door and sat on the ceramic floor near the drain. He took a deep breath, held the unit up to one of the small silver studs in his cheek and with a shaking hand, thumbed the unit on.

CHAPTER SEVENTEEN

FOR A CHANGE, Dex spent the morning focussed mainly on the work his employer paid him to do. At least, that was the way it appeared. While he answered customer questions and routinely tried to get them to buy more upgrades or newer packages, his mind was turning over the information about Luis Harker's death. The report indicated that a neuroscan was being done on the body for traces of stims or other pharma. Dex had asked the organization's system to alert him to any updates on the Harker file, so he'd find out when the results were in. Dex guessed that they would find something in the scan — he just couldn't imagine anyone happily undergoing torture like that without some kind of chemical assistance. Even if the man had somehow agreed to be flayed like that, the smile on his face just made no sense. But Dex knew there were powerful enough stims available that could block out anything.

Shortly after lunch, Dex had a ping on his private system. He expected it to be the automated response from the Cubicle Men's system with the chem report on Harker's body, but it wasn't. It was Annabelle.

"Hey, kiddo," Dex subvocalized, "you're not snowed under today?"

Annabelle ignored his question. "I've found Hazel's body."

Dex took a deep breath. He'd known that this would happen, had been waiting for it, but now that Annabelle had finally said those words, he found that he wasn't prepared for the reality of it.

He tamped down the feelings of nausea and got down to business. "Give me the details," he asked Annabelle, glad that speaking silently hid the roughness of his voice.

She sent him the coordinates and Dex overlaid them on a map of the city. The location was deep in brown sector, an area full of abandoned buildings in various states of dereliction. Most were used by unemployed squatters, but some were so bad that even they wouldn't live there. Dex knew there would be plenty of places to hide a body.

"What are you going to do?" Annabelle asked.

Dex thought for a fraction of a minute. "Okay," he said. "I've opened a case file on the system," and he sent her a link as they were speaking. "If you could do me a favour and add your information to the file." There was a pause as Annabelle scanned the report.

"You didn't mention that we know that Hazel is dead," she said, surprised.

"It wasn't an official case when you found that out," Dex said, sheepishly. "Zizou was on my ass about using resources without explaining why and I didn't want to involve you. The timeline on our end doesn't matter, so just don't put a date on when you learned that, okay?"

"Sure," Annabelle said, "but remember that I'm a big girl, Dex, and I'm perfectly happy to take responsibility for the things I do. If I help you, that's my choice. You don't need to protect me from anything."

"Okay," Dex said, but he doubted that he would have done it differently. There was no need for Annabelle to pay for his recklessness. "Anyway, once the information on the location of her body is in the system, just pipe the file over to Malone's team. They'll have someone go take a look today, I'm sure."

"It's done," Annabelle said, after hardly a beat had passed.

"That was fast," Dex said, impressed.

"You don't get to be a world class cracker with two jobs without being pretty quick." Annabelle said, a smile in her voice. "Speaking of which, I have to get back to it. We'll talk later, okay?"

"Definitely," Dex said. "You've been a big help, kiddo."

"Aw shucks," Annabelle said, laughing, as she ended the call.

• • •

Dex spent the rest of the afternoon jumpy and annoyed. He knew he couldn't do anything until the chem screen on Harker was in or the goons found Hazel's body and started that ball rolling. But it was maddening to have so much new information so close and yet so far away. Dex wished for the first time that he was still on the goon squad. He had no desire to see Hazel's dead body; rather the opposite. He was dreading the inevitable images and video that the squad would provide and that he would have to pore over. But he hated the waiting, relying on someone else to provide the intelligence he needed. It was incredibly frustrating and made him angry. He nearly yelled at two customers before taking a walk to the break room for a coffee and a chance to clear his head.

When the work day finally ended, Dex stormed out of the office complex. He logged into the Cubicle Men's system as soon as he was shot of the building's door and let his feet carry him to the train stop unaided by conscious vision. The screen on Harker still wasn't in, which he knew because he'd had no notification of it, but he thought there might be some news on Hazel's body. He paged over to the goon squad's area and watched the live feed of information from the folks on the street.

He scanned the rolling wave of words, much of it text extracted from audio as the squad members reported in from their rounds. He couldn't find anything in the current conversation about Hazel's body, so he ran a search over the last few hours for the location he'd described. Immediately his system showed him the hit — a request had been sent to the squad members closest to the area, Vonruden and Lino, to check it out on their shift. Dex focussed his system on their reports alone and saw that they were stuck mediating some dispute between a shopkeeper and a streeter. Dex didn't bother with the details, just saw that they guessed it would be at least thirty minutes before they were going to be free. By then, his stop had been reached and Dex automatically had begun walking toward his apartment building. He refocussed on his surroundings and made a decision.

He went up to his apartment, quickly changed out of his B&B uniform into nondescript street clothes and walked out of his apartment. He called up a city map and got directions to the location Annabelle had given him. It was a couple of trains to get there, but Dex figured he might even get to the spot before Vonruden and Lino arrived. He sent them both a quick, low priority message letting them know he was going to be there. He didn't know what either of them looked like in the flesh, since he'd only ever met them at the squad meetings held in M City and there was no reason to assume that their avatars looked anything like their physical selves. He sent them both an image of himself so they would recognize him.

He quickly updated the case file to indicate that he was going to the address in brown sector and shot a ping to Annabelle. He wanted to keep her informed of what was going on in the investigation, but really he just wanted someone to know where he was. He couldn't think of a reason why it would be dangerous, but he found that his heart was pounding. It had been a long time since he had been on the streets and he was nervous.

He switched trains at the edge of red sector, the main business area of the city. He caught the brown line and watched as the infrastructure of the city visibly deteriorated as it flashed past the train's grimy windows. The buildings in red sector were tall, shiny monoliths, symbols of the firms' control over the people and spaces of the city. Across the border, the complexes grew smaller, more squalid, more haphazard. The further the train travelled into brown sector, the less well kept the buildings became, until he was faced with literally crumbling apartment towers and broken down squats.

He could see from his map overlay that he was getting close to the building where Hazel's body was hidden. As the train slowed, he waited for the door to spiral open, then he jumped down to the platform. The train shushed away and he looked around. There weren't many people about on the street, though Dex guessed that many corners and doorways would have people sleeping or hanging around, just out of sight. He started walking down the street toward the building which was lit with a cool blue glow on his map overlay.

He couldn't see anyone hanging around the location where he expected to find Hazel's body. He logged into his account on the Cubicle Men's system and looked up Lino and Vonruden's reports. They had finally settled the dispute between the streeter who was trying to use a local hydro-farmer's storage room as a home and the owner of the space. They were headed to Dex's location now and Dex estimated that they would arrive in five minutes. He hoped that they would have had an opportunity to see his message — he didn't want to try to have to explain his presence if they didn't know who he was.

He sat on the curb and waited. The sun, such as it was, was going down, its light trapped behind the tall buildings which surrounded brown sector. Dex could see movement out of the corner of his eye, but every time he turned in its direction there was nothing there to be seen. It was disconcerting, but intellectually he knew not to be afraid. He knew that Vonruden and Lino were going to be there any minute; he also knew that almost everyone on the street was more afraid of a stranger than anything else. Plus, he'd pocketed the old knuckledusters he'd used those few years he spent on the streets. He was prepared if anything came up.

He hadn't waited long when he saw a man and a woman walking briskly down the street toward him. Dex didn't know what to expect from Melissa Vonruden and Eduardo Lino, but he was sure it was them. They were walking in the middle of the street, not trying to keep to the shadows or look for a way to escape should things get hairy. They both wore stunners on their belts and Dex was sure they each had at least one other weapon on their bodies. They exuded calm confidence, but they didn't seem like folks on a power trip to Dex. Some of the goon squad got that way, but Lino and Vonruden seemed all right. The tall woman waved as she approached Dex.

"You must be Andersson Dexter," she said, in a clear, strong voice. Dex stood as she stepped toward him, her hand extended. He clasped it and felt her firm grip as she shook his hand. "I'm Melissa Vonruden," she said and turned to her partner standing a few steps behind her. "This is Eduardo Lino." She introduced the man and he lifted a hand in greeting to Dex.

"You think there's a body in there?" Lino asked, gesturing to the crumbling building.

"Annabelle Lewis traced my missing person's ID chip to this location," Dex said and the two goons both nodded curtly.

"Okay," Vonruden said. "Let's go and take a look, shall we?"

CHAPTER EIGHTEEN

TALL, THIN MELISSA Vonruden led the three of them into the broken down old building. Dex, who was right behind her, watched as she slowly swept her eyes over the space while they slowly picked their way into the first room. "I'm sorry I didn't bring my old scanner from my days on the street," Dex said, "double up the effort."

"We don't use scanners anymore," Vonruden said, without turning back.

"She's got a Mark Four optical upgrade," Lino said, as if Dex was supposed to know what that meant. "I'll be getting mine in a couple of months," he added. Dex just nodded and guessed that Vonruden was using various kinds of vision enhancement, looking for dangers of the human, technological and physical kind. Just because they didn't see any people, that didn't mean they were alone in the room and it also didn't mean that someone hadn't left behind a little surprise to keep the space to themselves. Streeters were often quite technologically adept and old but still functional equipment was always available from street corner resellers for next to nothing. It wasn't unusual to find surprisingly complex booby traps in the seemingly abandoned buildings many streeters used as homes. And, of course, there were falling beams, broken floors and general debris to be concerned with. Dex was glad he had waited for help before heading in.

Annabelle's search program had turned up detailed coordinates for Hazel's body, so Dex and his two cohorts knew exactly where in the building to look. The problem, though, was figuring out how to get there. The body was in a subterranean room, close to the centre of the building, but there was no obvious way of getting to the floor below. Following Melissa Vonruden, Dex and Eduardo Lino stepped between broken furniture, old food brick wrappers and bits of hardware Dex couldn't even begin to identify. It was getting cold; there was obviously no heating in the building and whatever insulation the walls had once provided was gone with holes that had been punched into them. Dex wished he'd brought a warmer jacket.

"We need to find a way to get downstairs," Dex said.

"I'm trying to find a pole or something," Vonruden said, her eyes narrowed as she scrutinized the area. Dex stepped over a box and put his foot in a pile of soggy towels.

"Ugh," he said. "This place is a real hole."

"There's an awful lot of places like this around here," Eduardo Lino said. "This whole sector was abandoned by the firms about twenty years ago and only a handful of the buildings have been taken over by the folks trying to make a living outside the system. Even then, they usually only have so much left over for improvements. It's a pretty rough place to live, let me tell you."

"I think I've got something," Vonruden interrupted. "Over on the east wall, it looks like there's a door and a set of steps beyond it."

"I don't see anything that looks like a door," Lino said, squinting at the ancient sheetrock, plastered over with various artefacts from the years of squatters.

"Yeah," Vonruden said, "it's totally hidden among all the crap on the wall. But I'm sure it's there. Follow me."

They carefully picked their way over to the wall, which was covered in old posters, wallpaper and Dex thought it was maybe some kind of glue or gruel thrown on top of it all. As they got closer, they could see that under all the mess on the wall there was a small door concealing an opening. Vonruden peered at it closely, then lightly touched the right side. Nothing happened. She looked back at Dex and Lino, then roughly put her shoulder to the door. It popped open with a loud creak and they saw a set of steps leading down into darkness.

Eduardo Lino pulled a small disk out of one of his cavernous pockets, snapped its centre and it began to glow. It got brighter as Lino threw it through the doorway and down the stairs. By the time it hit the bottom, it was shining brightly and lit the stairwell. Vonruden looked back at the two men and started stepping down into the lower room. "It's a bit treacherous," she called back after having traversed a couple of the rickety metal steps. "But I think I can make it all the way down." Dex heard her heavy boots on the metal tread clunk down the steps, then stop with a soft thud. "Yeah," she shouted up, "it's no problem. I just need to get a little more light down here."

"I've got it," Lino said, pulling another couple of disks from his pockets, while he and Dex picked their way carefully down the stairs. After a flick of Lino's wrists, Dex saw two glowing shapes sail down into the room and then the whole place lit up from corner to corner. It was as bright as day down there, so none of them could miss the corpse lying in the middle of the floor.

• • •

Dex didn't want to get too close, but he couldn't keep away, either. He stepped up to the body, which had a bunch of small insects crawling on it. In what must have been shock, Dex found himself thinking that you didn't often see insects in the more built up areas of the city, probably because there was so little organic matter there. Why his mind went there he didn't know, but he did know that he really did not want to think about what he saw in that basement room. He let Lino and Vonruden do what needed to be done — the videos, still images and physical scans of the body and the area. They would need backup to move the body out of there, but they would have to get complete scans of the room first. Dex just stayed out of the way, trying not to think.

It was Hazel, of course. Her torso was dark with congealed blood and Dex thought he saw strips of skin hanging off. He couldn't tell if the front of her legs were cut or simply stained by the blood from her chest wounds, but he knew that Vonruden and Lino would get that information. All of a sudden, Dex wanted to be anywhere but at the scene. He stood against the stairs, breathing deeply and watching Lino and Vonruden work.

Vonruden stayed close to the body, using a sterile handheld scanner over every centimetre of Hazel's body. The scanner detected and logged data from trace evidence like hair and dust and took samples of Hazel's tissues. More information would come when Vonruden cut shallowly into Hazel's head to access the data port in her interface. Then they would have access to data on Hazel's physical condition — body tissue temperature and function, muscle action, just about anything that happened in or to Hazel's body would be recorded there. Between the external scans and that data, the autopsy software on the Cubicle Men's system would be able to provide an analysis of what happened to her.

Eduardo Lino was using a larger scanner on the room, walking a grid while waving the beam over the floor and walls. The device would identify and log any organic matter and could separate trace elements which were consistent with the environment from those which appeared to be introduced to the area. In a derelict building home to squatters for years, Dex wondered how useful that analysis could be. Even so, Lino methodically scanned the room.

Dex waited until Lino finished with the main part of the room and was coming over to scan the area where Hazel's body lay, then quietly interrupted.

"I, uh, don't need to be here any more, do I?" he asked and he saw Lino smile slightly.

"No," Vonruden said. "We could have handled it on our own all along. Everything we find will be in the report." Dex didn't think she was trying to be rude, simply stating a fact. He didn't really care either way.

"I knew her," Dex said quietly. "I had to know for sure."

"Understood," Lino said, gently. "But we've got it from here. Another crew is on its way to move the body and after that we'll start to have preliminary results. You can head on out anytime you want." He smiled at Dex and softly laid a hand on the man's shoulder. He gave a slight squeeze, then let his hand drop back by his side.

"Thanks," Dex said, heat radiating through his body from the shoulder down. He couldn't even remember the last time he'd felt another person's touch like that. It was emotional and personal, not like shaking hands or jostling on the train. It made Dex's head swim even more than the dark room and stench of death. He fled up the stairs, so quickly he almost lost his footing on one of the warped treads. As he scrambled out the door and into the main room of the building, he brought his hand to his face to discover that his cheeks were wet.

•••

The train rides back to his neighbourhood were a blur. He stumbled into his apartment and barely made it to the lav before he threw up. He leaned against the wall, heaving for a moment, before finally getting a grip on himself and slugging back a shot of FlyingFish. His stomach settled and he walked back to his room. He stuffed his clothes in the autoclave, pulled out a food brick and the bottle of rum. He ate a bit of the gooey meal and poured a large shot into his glass. He sat down and sipped the drink.

He knew Hazel was dead before he got to the scene and even though he had no real evidence to connect Hazel's death with Luis Harker's, he had been expecting the mutilation. But he was still shaken. There hadn't been many bodies when he was on the goon squad and most of those had been fresh. Still, Dex knew it was because he knew her that this one hit hard. It was the first time he'd seen the dead body of someone he knew.

He was halfway through the Jamaica's Best and doing a good number on staring at the wall, when he registered a noise in the back of his mind. After a moment, he realized that it was a ping from his system. He had an incoming message. He wasn't ready to see the report from Vonruden and Lino; Hazel was already dead, what difference would another few hours make? He was going to ignore it, then for some reason he switched his head up display on. It wasn't the report; it was Annabelle.

Dex answered. "We got Hazel's body."

"I saw the live report," Annabelle said. "You were there?"

"Yeah," Dex sighed. "It was a mistake. They didn't need me, I was just in the way. And I wish I hadn't seen her—" His voice broke.

Annabelle filled the silence. "I'm sorry, Dex," she said. "This is a tough one, for sure. Was it... was it bad?"

"Bad enough," he answered. "You remember the body they found last week, down in brown sector?"

"Sure," Annabelle said. "What about it?"

"What happened to Hazel looked an awful lot like what happened to him."

"You're sure?" Annabelle asked.

"Pretty sure," Dex said. "I'm waiting on the scans from the other body and of course for the stuff on Hazel, but I think we've got something serious here."

He waited for Annabelle to answer. She took her time. "You think this is murder," she said and it didn't sound like a question.

"I'm keeping an open mind," Dex said. "It could be a kinky sensation thing gone wrong, or some kind of weird side effect of some stim or 'buzzer. But the Harker scene definitely had indications that one or more other persons were involved and that always makes me suspicious. And I can say that Hazel might have been into stims, but I never saw physical wounds or bruises on her. If she was doing sensation thrills, it was well hidden, which usually means well controlled."

"But, you don't think that's what it is, do you?" Annabelle asked. "If you were pressed, you'd say they were murdered."

"If I had to bet," Dex said, swallowing the last of his drink, "I'd say we have a serial killer loose on brown sector."

CHAPTER NINETEEN

THE WORK DAY at Barrett and Brar was a wash for Dex. He somehow managed to get the minimum number of tasks done and no one seemed to notice that he was in a daze the whole time. Part of him wanted to spend the day online, poring over the now complete report on Luis Harker and the preliminary work on Hazel. But he knew that there was no way he could focus on that data while under the watchful eyes of B&B's bosses. Usually he was a master at appearing to work while really busy on other activities, but he knew that this day he wouldn't be able to hide. He also was feeling a bit the worse for wear, having talked to Annabelle for an hour, then taking a few more medicinal Jamaica's Bests. It would have to wait for the end of the day and the coming three days off.

Once he was finally back at his apartment, Dex changed and got his supplies ready — a jug of water, a stack of food bricks and pillow for the chair. He ate while he logged in to the Cubicle Men's system and quickly scanned his messages. There was nothing surprising, just the automated notification about the Harker report and a message from Eduardo Lino letting Dex know that they'd finished with the scene and that Hazel's body had been taken to B&B. As her employer, they were responsible for disposal of her body. The techs at B&B told Lino that there was no next of kin listed in her personal file, so she would be torched later that day. Dex fired back a quick auto-acknowledgment, just letting Lino know he'd read the message but had nothing to add. Then he paged over to the preliminary report on Hazel.

She had been cut, in a similar style to the wounds on Luis Harker, but there were several apparent differences. All of the severed strips of skin were still at the scene and the cuts themselves were much less straight and even than they had been on Harker's body. Also, there were many fewer incisions — none on Hazel's legs and only three separate cuts on her torso. She had still bled and bled enough that blood loss was listed as the probable cause of death. The neuro scans were still outstanding, which would show more specifically the physiological processes that occurred immediately prior to death. Without that detailed information, though, loss of blood seemed the likely cause.

Dex didn't even bother with the images of the body. He had seen enough the previous day and he just wasn't prepared to go through that again. Not yet. Maybe in a day or two, once the shock of it had faded and Dex could start to treat this just like any other case, he would go through all the evidence again, but it just wasn't something he was ready to tackle yet.

He paged over to the complete report on Harker's body. The marks on Harker's wrists did not match the slight lesions on his upper arms and torso, however they had been made at the same time. The wrists showed a pattern of a particular brand of restraints marketed to Security branches called Hold-Alls. He'd never heard of them before, guessing that they were relatively new on the market, but Dex ran a quick search and saw that they were easily available for purchase by anyone. Plenty of people were into sensation play and restraints were as popular as they had ever been for that kind of thing. In less than a minute, Dex had found a half dozen online retailers selling the things. He didn't fancy his chances looking for recent buyers.

He moved on to the marks on Harker's arms and torso. Those

had been made by polymer rope, probably looped around the man's body a couple of times then tied off. There were indications of abrasion, as if he had struggled against his bindings. The report added, though, that the amount of abrasion was consistent with less than a minute of moderate movement against the rope. Dex doubted that what had been done to Luis Harker could have been accomplished in less than a minute, so for some reason the man had stopped struggling early on. Maybe he had lost consciousness, or been stunned or electrically immobilized. Dex moved on to the neuroscan report, looking for answers.

There was an indication that a low level stunner or electro-compliance tool had been used, but according to the scan, its effects had worn off well before the cutting started. Harker had most certainly been conscious until the moment of his death, which was listed conclusively as exsanguination — he bled to death. There was, however, a huge spike in naturally occurring dopamine and endorphins in Harker's system. It was a larger surge than was consistent with normal production during peak pleasure experiences, so it was unlikely that Harker was simply getting off on the cutting. In fact, it was a vastly larger amount than the human body usually would produce naturally. The report speculated that some kind of physical neurostimulant could be used to force production of those chemicals and Dex ran a cross search for the concept while he finished reading the report.

The auto-generated report was designed to be careful not to draw conclusions, but Dex didn't have those constraints. He was certain that Harker had been held against his will, then had something done to him to make him compliant. The neurochems in the body were almost certainly delivered or triggered by an outside agent. Also, marks on his arms and wrists did indicate that there had been a struggle at some point in the proceedings, which made it unlikely that the episode had been consensual. And Dex had a feeling in his gut that this was a killer. The same killer who took Hazel to that hell-ish room, drugged and cut her.

He paged over to the search results and saw that there was a device you could buy which used electrical impulses to stimulate implanted nodes into forcing production of various neurochems. They were mostly used to simulate pleasure, but they could be pro-grammed for anything. They functioned as light stunners or pain-sticks as well and Dex found several boards devoted to their use and configuration. There were a couple of different manufacturers branding the things as Joybuzzers or Stimsticks and it looked like the devices, while expensive, were easy to come by. Another dead end, Dex figured. At least he was starting to piece together a plausi-ble scenario of how the killer had done it.

The killer had lured Harker into the room, or grabbed him off the street, subduing him with a stunner jolt from the Stimstick. Then Dex figured that the wrist restraints had come out and he'd been tied further with the polymer rope. He'd come to while bound and before the killer could administer the Stimstick again, this time with its pleasure creating feature, Harker had struggled in his bonds, creating the wounds Dex saw on the man's wrists, arms and torso. Dex wondered if the cutting started before or after the Stimstick was used the second time. He hoped it was after.

Dex went back over the report on Harker's wounds. He had assumed that the killer used a laser cutter, but the report indicated that the weapon had been, in fact, a steel blade. Tiny fragments of steel had been found along the edges of the wounds and the cuts were not consistent with the clean, cauterizing beam of a laser. Dex was surprised. Steel knives were not common and the use of the Stimsticks make Dex think that the killer was not averse to modern conveniences. He thought about the dichotomy — the killer was happy to use brand new wrists restraints and Stimsticks, but the cutting was done with an ancient tool. Dex guessed that there must be something special about the knife. He wondered if there was any way to trace the blade.

He ran a search on the Cubicle Men's system for any information on steel blades and on a hunch, on any deaths that were similar to Harker's and Hazel's. It would be a while before the results were in, so Dex refocussed on his apartment for a few moments. He stood, worked the kinks out of his neck and stretched. He visited the lav and refilled his jug of water. He was feeling like a human being again and didn't have to go in to B&B for another three days. Three days of blissful relief from the boredom and banality of answering customer enquiries for things that no one needed anyway. Dex pulled down the bottle of Jamaica's Best and a container of gingapop. He mixed a drink and took a sip.

Back in the chair, he accessed his personal system and dimmed the lights in his apartment slightly. He sent a ping to Annabelle and when she answered asked if she wanted to go out. "I've spent the night with the reports on Hazel and the other victim," he said, "and I could use a change of scenery."

"So they are related?" Annabelle asked.

"I think so," Dex said. "I'll know more when the full scan on Hazel comes in, but it really looks like they were both murdered."

Annabelle let out a breath. "Murdered," she repeated.

"Again, it's not certain," Dex said, hedging.

"But you think they were murdered," Annabelle said and it didn't sound like a question.

"Yeah," Dex said. "There's no doubt another person was involved, almost certainly the cutter and there's good evidence on the Harker body that he was coerced at a very minimum. Like I said, I'll know more when the scan comes in on Hazel." He took a sip of his drink, then said, "but I'm sure you'd rather get out of the house to have this conversation, so let's go somewhere."

"Sure," Annabelle said, "I don't have much in the morning — I can afford to be a little out of it tomorrow."

"Aw, shit," Dex said, "I forgot that we're not on the same week schedule. I'm on weekend now."

"Yeah," Annabelle said. "I still have a day. But then I'm coming over for Pat Malone's retirement, so that will be good at least."

"It sure will," Dex said. "So, you're still up for heading out?"

"Sure," Annabelle said. "Meet you in Monte's?"

"You bet," Dex said and ended the call.

CHAPTER TWENTY

DEX LINKED INTO Monte's as soon as he ended the call with Annabelle. He used to come here even before he started seeing her. He didn't think of it as the same as really going out — it was just something to look at other than the four bleak walls of his apartment, like some folks watched vids or played games. They offered a good set of canned music at Monte's; there were usually four or five playlists to choose from and Dex often was spoiled for choice. Other people were good about leaving you alone there, too, but in a pinch he could usually find someone from the squad hanging around in the joint if he needed a conversation.

He had sometimes wondered if spending time at Monte's was a way to help him get used to the virtual world, or if it actually made it harder for him to integrate into the online community. Monte's, while obviously part of M City, felt more like a throwback to the online world Dex grew up with, a world where you could socialize or not on your own terms; where no one, other than an admin, knew you were there unless you made yourself known; where you were essentially alone, just alone with most of the rest of the known world.

His thoughts were interrupted as Annabelle materialized at Dex's table, looking beautiful as always, even though she wore just her simple outfit of brown pants and a shirt patterned with some old painting on it. She had a whole wardrobe of them and Dex had given up trying to identify each piece. He thought this one might be a Mondrian, but art was never his strong suit.

She pecked his cheek and slid into the booth beside him. "Hey, handsome," she said, her voice low even though they were on a private voice channel and no one else could hear them.

Dex chuckled and said, "Hey, yourself. You've sure got a funny sense of aesthetics, but I guess anyone could tell that just by looking at your chest." He gestured at the red, black and white squares and rectangles of her shirt. "There are two things in this world I will never understand — art and what a wonderful woman like you sees in a cantankerous old man like me."

Annabelle giggled and slid her avatar a little closer to Dex's. He didn't have a full body simulation activated, so he couldn't feel it, but he could see what she was doing. He was pleased to notice that it hadn't started to bother him yet. "Art, beauty, porn — it's all the same," Annabelle said, "you can't define it, you just know it when you see it." She beamed up at Dex and he smiled in both the virtual and physical worlds.

He slipped an arm around her, grateful that he couldn't feel the jarring sensation of simulated touch and sighed happily. "Aw, kiddo," he said, shaking out a cigarette with his free hand, "I needed this tonight. What a godawful couple of days it's been. I just feel old, useless and tired."

"You're not that old," Annabelle said, suddenly serious. She pulled away from his embrace and looked him in the face. "I mean, I've never asked, but you just don't seem that old."

Dex had stopped paying complete attention to the avatars and was missing Annabelle's concern. "I feel ancient, kiddo," he said, sighing deeply. "One step away from decay."

"Damn it, Dex," Annabelle said, raising her voice and forcing his attention back to the representation of them both. "Do I have to be planning your retirement party soon? Are you going to wake up some morning next year or, christ, next week with wrinkles and bad knees? I need to know."

Dex looked at her and was surprised to see the concern on her face. He had been unfair, he knew, complaining when he was miles away from old age. He tried to soften his face and said, "Honey, I'm sorry. Full disclosure: I'm 68 years old."

Annabelle's face relaxed visibly. "Damn it, you scared me. Here I was, all of a sudden terrified that you were on the south side of a hundred and I had to start worrying about you falling apart any day now. Thank you. I'm glad to know that there's a few klicks left on you yet." She beamed at him.

"Glad to appease," he said. "Now, I know it's impolite to ask a lady her age, but I do feel that turn around is fair play."

"I hope you don't think you're robbing the cradle," she said, coyly. "But I only turned fifty-five a couple of months ago."

"My god," Dex said, mock mortified, "you're just a child! I've been corrupting a minor. Whatever will I do?" They both laughed and another drink appeared in front of Annabelle.

"This will have to be my last," she said, lifting the glass to her lips, "I do need to work tomorrow."

"I shall have you in bed by midnight," Dex said, gallantly.

"If only that were so," Annabelle muttered to herself as she took a sip of the stim cocktail.

• • •

They stayed at Monte's another half hour, talking about anything but the case. Annabelle linked out and Dex found himself awake and uninterested in just staring at his apartment or forcing himself to sleep. He pulled a schedule from The Dog and Pony, hoping there would be a decent band. He didn't recognize the name of the group playing, but decided it didn't matter. He linked over and listened as he materialized to a wailing horn overlaid with some kind of tribal rhythm. It was odd, but it would do. He found a table near the back and sat.

The music washed over him and after a couple of songs Dex had forgotten all about the case. He had forgotten about most everything — his job at B&B, his work with the Cubicle Men, the struggles he and Annabelle were having. He was simply buoyed along by the music. The band was a three piece: a pair of horn players and a seemingly multi-armed drum machine operator. The horns were fabulous, long and loud and very analog sounding. Dex wondered how the virtual instruments got that sound — he liked to think that he could tell the real thing on a recording and this sounded like the real thing. If the horn players were swinging, the drummer was rocking. He was waving his arms around like crazy, moving from drum machine to synth and sample deck and back again. It was a strange counterpoint to the crooning horns, but it sounded great.

In the break between the sets, Dex made his way up to the stage and cornered one of the horn players. "That was great," he said to the strange looking avatar. It was nominally female shaped, but very tall and large, with a wolf's head. He had seen stranger avatars, but it was still a little unusual.

"Thanks," a melodious but androgynous voice said.

"That really sounds like a physical trumpet," Dex said, feeling foolish. "I've never heard a virtual horn like that."

"I expect it will be a long time before you do," the trumpeter said. "It is a real trumpet. Both the trombone and I play in the physical world and pump the sound through to here."

"Wow," Dex said. "Are you playing a gig out there, too?"

"Not today," the musician said. "But sometimes we do. Double the exposure, right?"

"Right," Dex said. "Well, that's all I wanted to say. You all are really tight."

"I appreciate it," the sultry voice said. The wolf's head cocked a little at Dex, then he thought he saw the mouth curl into a smile. "Didn't I see you playing here last Thursday? Celestial Chemical, isn't it?"

"Chemical Celeste, actually," Dex said, grinning. "It was our first gig. I hope we didn't stink up the joint too much."

"Not at all," the wolf's head said. "I seem to remember you started out pretty tentatively, but pulled it together right off. It was good. You're the mandolin, right?"

"Yup," Dex said, beaming.

"You play out there?"

"I used to," Dex said, "a long time ago. And I just started again. It's coming back, but slower than I'd like."

"Yeah, it's like that," the wolf said. "Well, don't give up; you guys were good."

"Thanks," Dex said and turned back to his table. He spent the next set thinking about Chemical Celeste and wondering about the logistics of feeding the sound from a real instrument into M City. He was sure he didn't have the equipment, but that was easy to change.

He stayed until the music was over, then logged out of M City. He fell into bed, buzzed on rum and music, and managed not to think about death, neurostims, blood or steel blades even once.

CHAPTER TWENTY-ONE

DEX SLEPT IN. He normally had his apartment turn off its waking settings for his weekends, but he was usually up within an hour or two of his typical wake up time anyway. Not this day. It was approaching noon when Dex finally opened his eyes. He didn't notice the time at first and just went about his usual morning routine, but when he was siting down to a cup of coffee and a breakfast bar, he went online and nearly choked when the clock appeared on his display.

He took a second to panic, then realized that he had nothing urgent to do. It felt urgent, working on the case of Hazel and Luis Harker's killings, but they were already dead and no amount of speed was going to change that. Dex guessed that the if the killer had struck twice, there was a good chance that more killing would follow, but he wasn't sure he could prove that Hazel and Harker were murdered, let alone figure out who did it and stop them from doing it again. As wrong as it felt, there was really no reason why Dex couldn't sleep until noon if he wanted to.

Now that he was awake, though, he wanted to get cracking. He logged into the Cubicle Men's system and paged over to the complete report on Hazel's scan. He skimmed it, looking for what he expected would be the similarities to Harker's killing. There they were — an electrical neurochemical stimulator was used, the cutting weapon was a steel-edged blade, Hold-Alls and polymer rope were used to bind her. This was enough, Dex knew. These two cases were obviously related. He sent a merge request to the Cubicle Men's system to create a new case file which combined all information on both cases. It also automatically scanned for similarities and differences and Dex would review that report when it was done, in case he'd missed something.

While he waited, he went through the report on Hazel's scan again, this time he read it word for word.

Neuro-physical scan on deceased Hazel Ramer case # 234857-AD
Time of death, physical: approx. 0200-0400 UTC
Time of death, neuro: 0307 UTC
Primary cause of death: Exsanguination
Other contributing factors: None
Toxicology: No foreign chemicals found in blood or tissue
Neurochemistry: Extremely high dopamine and endorphin levels; evidence of excessive node stimulation on two facial nodes from a single high power blast; delivery system unknown
Physical state: Three long longitudinal shallow lacerations on torso (epidermal layer breached, muscle layer intact), two approximately 120 cm^2 patches of skin removed, but still attached to the body; microscopic fragments of steel found in the wounds; ligature marks on both wrists, consistent with Hold-All brand restraints; ligature marks on upper arms and upper torso, consistent with three strands of polymer rope; light bruising on back in two parallel horizontal lines, consistent with consistent pressure with 2 cm diameter round objects
Notes:
1. Lacerations made within one hour of death.
2. Ligature marks made within one hour of death.
3. Ligature marks indicate very little movement of subject against restraints.
4. Neurochemical level inconsistent with natural production.
5. Neurochemical level inconsistent with chemical stimulation.
6. Lacerations consistent with cuts by steel blade, approx. 0.5-1 mm in width, 10-20 cm in length.
7. EXCEPTION: Neurochemical level inconsistent with any known physical stimulation, however evidence of facial node stimulation indicates physical stimulation.

Dex's eyes were drawn to the red exception at the end of the report. This was different from Harker's report, where the scan determined that the neurochemical level in Harker's system was consistent with known physical stimulators. Something had changed between Harker's death and Hazel's killing and Dex wondered if that would be the break he needed. The Stimstick was the key. Dex hadn't fancied his chances of finding the killer through purchase records, but now he wasn't so sure if this was something so new that the scans didn't recognize it. He sent a request to the system to trace all orders of both brands of node stimulators. He also sent a similar request for a list of purchasers of Hold-Alls restraints. He set the system to cross reference both lists and show Dex the names which were on both lists.

In the meantime, he ran a search for new or upgraded Stimsticks. He started by looking for information on the two brands of neurochemical stimulators. They seemed to be fairly similar, though the Joybuzzer brand was marketed specifically as a pleasure enhancer, while Stimsticks clearly had the potential to be used for multiple purposes. Dex drilled down into the technical details, though, and discovered that both devices were essentially the same in construction. He wasn't entirely sure that both devices could be used as a stunner, but a quick search of some the boards for users of both tools made it clear that they were multipurpose.

There were some rumours of a new version of the Joybuzzer product, but like most online rumours, there was more speculation than information. Dex guessed that there really was a new product coming and he wondered if that was what the killer had used on Hazel. The existing products were apparently easy to modify, though, so it was possible that the killer hadn't actually changed tools. Dex didn't know enough about these things to be sure. He would need outside help and he didn't think Annabelle would be able to sort it out for him this time.

• • •

Pat Malone's retirement party was coming up the following night and Dex could ask around then. He knew that shop talk was inevitable at these things, so he would hopefully find someone who knew more about how these things worked and where they could be found. Thinking about Malone's party reminded Dex that he needed to book a room for Annabelle. If they had been a different kind of couple, she would probably just stay with Dex, even though there was barely enough room for him in the small apartment, but as it was there was no way that she would be able to stay there for any length of time. It was hard enough for the two of them to be in the apartment together for an hour or more.

Dex hated that Annabelle stayed in a guesthouse when she visited, but he was still amazed that she visited at all. Their visits were always strange and awkward. Annabelle was trying, there was no way to deny that, but Dex could tell that every inch of her screamed to get away when they were together. She was one of those people who had always felt out of place and uncomfortable in the physical world, so escaped to the online communities. When Marionette City was realized, those people tended to move lock stock and barrel into the virtual world, conducting every activity they could online. This was Annabelle.

In M City, she was a strong, gregarious woman, competent and bright. She was social, funny and outgoing. In the physical world, though, she was painfully shy, terribly unhappy in the company of other people. Although she was better when it was just the two of them, he found that it was like being with another person, though there was now a spark of her real personality shining through. Dex wondered how she would handle Pat Malone's party. He was still shocked that she'd said she would make an appearance.

He booked a room for her at the usual spot, the Red Fish Inn, a reasonably inexpensive small hotel two blocks away from Dex's apartment. The rooms there were slightly smaller than Dex's apartment, but they were modern, spotless and some even sported a view of the postage stamp sized neighbourhood park. Annabelle liked it there and it allowed them to spend as much time together as was feasible, given the circumstances. Given the cost of the jet flight from Nice, it was a drop in the bucket and Annabelle did quite well between her day job and her work for The Cubicle Men. She certainly never complained about the cost.

Dex sent her the confirmation and then checked his messages for details about Malone's party. It was set for seven pm and the address for the pub was given along with a map. It would be a quick train ride to the pub, which was in a reasonably good part of green sector. Dex had worked in the area when he was with the goons and it had been fairly rough then. In the intervening years plenty had changed and the area had become a favourite for the young and differently employed. The rise of M City as a recreational centre also created a new economy, which was outside the control of the firms. There were now entire industries which existed solely in M City, with thousands of people working only for cash. Those people needed housing and other real world goods, but they had real cash to pay for them, too. A lot of previously bad neighbourhoods had been turned over to these independents and apartments were fixed up and even complexes built in some places.

Since so many of these people were outsiders, they also attracted the artsy crowd, who lived off their leavings. Dex knew that much of green sector would be familiar to him, as he'd lived in places like that for many years. This pub that Malone's party was going to be at, The Cog and Sprocket, was doubtlessly going to be like any number of places where Dex used to shine the bar. Dex hadn't been back to a place like that since he decided to go legit and get a job back in his mid thirties. Part of him was nervous to walk back into that life, but part of him was looking forward to the realness of it all.

He almost wished Annabelle weren't going to be there.

CHAPTER TWENTY-TWO

ANNABELLE ARRIVED EARLY the next afternoon. Dex had taken the train to the airport to meet her at the gate and he was struck dumb when he saw her spiral down the pole from the arrivals area. She looked so beautiful — she had done something new to herself since he'd seen her in Nice. Was it her hair? Dex thought it looked somehow more luminescent. Her baby blues shone out from under the glinting fringe on her forehead and Dex marvelled that for someone who wished she could just disappear, Annabelle certainly knew how to light up a room.

Dex was careful to restrain himself when they met. He let her take the lead as she walked up to him. She tentatively tilted her head up toward his and they kissed lightly. This was only the second time she had let him get that close to her and Dex thought the whole airport could hear his heart jackhammering in his chest. He let her pull away and took her bags.

"I can carry them just fine," Annabelle said. "The antigrav chips work perfectly well in here."

"You've got to let me at least try to be a gentleman," Dex said, grinning. "Maybe if I'm lucky the floor on the way to the train will have demagnetized and I'll really have to lug these around." He hefted her two small bags, one in each hand, as if they were heavy.

"Okay, fine," Annabelle said. "If you want to be a big brute, I'm not going to stop you."

"Me big strong man," Dex said and grunted. Annabelle laughed and walked alongside him as they made their way to the train stop.

After the short ride in, Dex checked her in to her room at the Red Fish Inn, then they went back to his apartment. Annabelle was being a good sport, but Dex could tell that she was anxious. "Having second thoughts?" he asked when she was sitting in his good chair and he was across the room perched on the side of the bed.

"About you?" she asked, nervously.

"No," Dex said softly, wondering all of a sudden if there was more to her skittishness than worrying about the event that evening. "Second thoughts about going to Malone's party."

"Maybe," she admitted. "It seemed like a good idea at the time." She smiled weakly.

"I know you've been doing so much better out here than you were," Dex said, a gentle smile on his face, "but maybe it's too much, too soon. I mean there will be an awful lot of people there and I doubt that the space will be very big. It could get pretty cramped in there."

"Yeah, I know," Annabelle said, looking at the floor. "I really want to be there for Pat, though."

"Were you close?" Dex asked, realizing that he had no idea if she and Malone were friends. For all he knew, they'd been an item at some point. Dex sometimes forgot that not everyone lived as solitary a life as he did.

"Kind of," she said, relaxing slightly into the chair. "You know how everyone in the organization is supposed to start as part of a street team?"

"Sure," Dex said.

"Well, I didn't really want to do that, as I'm sure you can guess." Dex smiled at her. "Anyway, I explained things to Pat and he was very kind to me. He helped me talk to Zizou and they let me in without having to do a tour on the streets. We've been friendly ever since."

"I'm not surprised they bent the rules for you, kiddo," Dex said. "You're so damn smart and it's not like people with skills like yours are falling out of the sky. They needed you a lot more than they needed to follow some dumb rules."

Annabelle smiled. "That may or may not be true, Mr. Flattery Will Get You Anywhere, but Pat went out of his way for me and I really don't want to miss his party. I know it's just a question of will-power; mind over matter."

"I think it's technically mind over mind, don't you think?" Dex said.

"You really can be pedantic, you know," Annabelle said, laughing. Dex was glad to hear that sound. He missed it so much when they were together in the physical world.

"So, what do you want to do?" Dex asked.

"I want to go, I just don't know how long I'll be able to handle it," she said, looking down at her lap.

"Why don't we turn up fairly early?" Dex suggested. "Hopefully it will be quieter, fewer people."

Annabelle nodded. "Good idea. I'll be able to talk to Pat without too much competition. I'll stay as long as I can, but I don't think I'll be in it for the long haul."

"Just let me know whenever you want to leave and we'll make our tree act." Dex said.

"You don't have to leave with me," Annabelle said, "I don't want to spoil your fun."

"Kiddo," Dex said, his voice low, "you are my fun."

Annabelle smiled, a little sadly. "You are a sweetheart," she said, "but honestly I might be better off on my own. I think we'll just have to play it by ear."

"Okay," Dex said. "It's your call." They sat, Dex looking at Annabelle while she kept her gaze out the small window.

"So, now that that's out of the way," Dex said, forcing his voice to be light, "what should we get Pat for a retirement gift? There will be plenty of real ale at the pub, so that's not the best choice."

"He likes Scotch, too," Annabelle said. "The real stuff, imported from Europa."

Dex whistled low. "Good thing you're made of cash," he said, "that stuff costs a fortune."

Annabelle grinned. "If you go out and get it, I'll split it with you fifty-fifty."

"You drive a hard bargain, woman," Dex said. "Luckily, I'm a stereotypical cop and I know of a real liquor store in town; I'll just check to make sure they have some in stock." He took on the thousand metre stare people get when they are going online and looked up the place. They had two different kinds of real whisky in stock and Dex had a bottle of the Glenross put aside for him. He logged off and said, "It's going to take me about a half hour to get there, so do you want to hang out here or head back to your hotel until it's time to go?"

"I don't mind staying here," Annabelle said, "if it's okay with you."

"I like having you here," Dex said, his voice soft. Annabelle glanced up at him, flushed and looked away. "Okay, I'll be back in ninety minutes or so."

"See you," Annabelle said, as Dex walked out the door.

• • •

Dex returned just over an hour later, with only a very expensive bottle of amber fluid in his arms. He'd had to restrain himself from buying one of the bottles of 7 year old rum the place stocked — he wasn't poor by any manner of means, but one bottle of the stuff cost three days salary and he just couldn't justify that kind of a purchase. It was awfully tempting, though.

He stepped into the apartment and saw Annabelle in more or less the same position she'd been in when he left. She was obviously online and Dex tried not to disturb her. He stowed the Scotch in the food cupboard, then he slipped into the lav. The autoclave had an access port from inside the tiny room, so he could stuff his clothes into it without bothering Annabelle. He showered quickly and pulled out some clothes from the small cupboard access in the room. He was amazed how this tiny apartment had all the necessary features for two people to share the space. Even Dex couldn't imagine living there full time with another person.

He dressed and tidied the lav, then stepped out of the small room. Annabelle was focussed on the apartment and she grinned at Dex as he emerged from the room. "You sure do clean up well," she said, her voice loose and easy.

"It helps to have a reason," Dex said, smiling and walked over to the cupboard. He took down the bottle of Scotch and showed Annabelle. "This is where all your money has gone," he said. "Take a good look, because that's all you'll get to do."

"Pat might share it," she said, dubiously.

"If he does, he's insane," Dex said. "I came perilously close to buying a seven year old bottle of rum in that store and I wouldn't share it with anyone. Well, I'd offer to share it with you, but only because I know you wouldn't want it."

Annabelle laughed. "I'm happy to stick with the neurostims," she said. "I had a snort while you were gone; I hope you don't mind. I figured it wouldn't hurt to get a little loose before the party, you know, build a little fuzzy wall between me and reality."

"I know exactly what you mean," Dex said, pulling down the bottle of Jamaica's Best. "This stuff bears about as much resemblance to that bottle of seven year old as I do to an elephant, but needs must when the devil drives." He poured a small shot into a glass, topped it off with a splash of water then toasted Annabelle. She raised an empty hand in return and Dex downed the drink. He grimaced, then said, "Nothing like getting a little head start, eh?"

"You are so strange," Annabelle said, laughing.

Dex bowed theatrically and said, "You wouldn't have me any other way, I'm sure."

"No," Annabelle said, "no, I wouldn't. Okay, let's go and get this over with."

"A more rousing pre-party speech has never been heard by man or beast," Dex said, as they left the apartment.

CHAPTER TWENTY-THREE

THE PUB WAS dark and small, but Dex's guess had been right and there were only a handful of people in the place. The invitation had included an image of Pat Malone for those who had only ever met the man in M City and Dex could see that he was sitting on a stool at the long bar, chatting with a man Dex recognized, but couldn't quite name. Both of them had tall glasses of dark beer in front of them on the wood-image panelled bar. He glanced back at Annabelle and saw that she was still smiling as she slowly moved deeper into the bar. She caught up with him and they walked together to the man of the hour.

"Pat," Annabelle said, leaning in to plant a light kiss on the older man's cheek.

"Annabelle Lewis, I presume," Malone said, a mixture of surprise and genuine joy in his voice. "You made it. I know it wasn't easy..."

"I said I'd be here, didn't I?" Annabelle chided. "Besides, flights are cheap right now." She grinned and Malone smiled back, obviously remembering that Annabelle had had to overcome more than mere distance to be there. Malone turned to Dex and clasped his hand warmly.

"It's good to see you, Dex" Malone said. "I'd recognize you anywhere." He grinned and jerked his head toward Annabelle. "That's some woman you've got yourself."

"Don't I know it," Dex said, smiling. "So let me get a taste of this incredible brew they've got here." Malone looked up and waved his arm at the man behind the bar. The barman came over and Dex ordered a pint of the house special. He turned to Annabelle, who shook her head and Dex asked for a soda water for her.

Malone raised an eyebrow when Dex passed the water over to Annabelle, but didn't say anything. "Don't want to mix my uppers and downers," Annabelle said, smiling, as she raised her glass. Dex lifted his frothy ale and they clinked glasses with Malone.

Dex turned to the other man sitting with Malone. He looked familiar but in the dim light Dex couldn't recognize him. He was about to introduce himself, when the man said, "Andersson Dexter,"

"Yeah," Dex said and stuck out his hand.

"Eduardo Lino," the other man said, shaking Dex's hand. "Good to see you again."

"You too," Dex said. "I didn't recognize you in civvies." Lino was dressed in a bright one-piece that Dex guessed cost more than that bottle of seven year old rum. "I never thanked you and your partner for your help the other day."

"It was nothing," Lino said. "You know, it's just what we do on street."

"Yeah," Dex said, "but you don't always have a soft old detective looking over your shoulder and getting all woozy at the sight of blood."

Lino laughed. "You were fine," he said. "I remember my first stiff — I spewed all over the scene. It's a good thing Malone here didn't find out, or I'd have been out on my ear."

Malone was talking to Annabelle, but looked over to the two men. "I heard that," he said, sternly, "and if you really think I didn't know about that incident with the Maxwell body, you're a long way from making detective squad, Lino." He grinned at the younger man, who raised his glass in a silent toast to his outgoing boss.

Malone turned back to Annabelle and Lino asked Dex, "So, what is going on with that? I've been following the case file and I saw that you merged it with the other body we found last week. You think they're related?"

"No doubt about it," Dex said. "Hey, speaking of which, do you know anything about physical neurostims?"

"I know what they are," Lino said, "but that's about it. However, I do know someone who knows a hell of a lot about those kind of things."

"Who?" Dex asked.

"Melissa," Lino said.

"Melissa..." Dex tried to put a face to the name.

"Vonruden, my partner," Lino said, laughing. "She works in a stim joint. She's got all the inside dope on that stuff. They don't handle online delivery, though, if that's what you need."

"Nope," Dex said, smiling. "I just need to know about the physical stuff; Stimsticks, Joybuzzers, that kind of thing. So, is she planning on coming out tonight, or should I just message her in the morning?"

"I'm pretty sure she's going the be here, but probably not until later," Lino said. "She's a bit of a night hawk."

"Great," Dex said. "Thanks for the help. Again."

"No problem," Lino laughed. "I'm happy to do it." He drained the last of his beer and gestured to the barman for another.

"I've got that one," Dex called to the bartender, as he was filling Lino's glass. He turned to Lino. "Least I can do."

The other man smiled. "Not necessary, but very much appreciated." Dex grinned and turned back to Malone. He saw that several other people had arrived in the pub and looked around for Annabelle. He couldn't see her.

"Oh shit," he muttered.

"What's that?" Malone asked, turning to Dex.

"Annabelle's gone," he said, miserably.

"No, she isn't," Malone said. "She's over there talking to Zizou." He pointed at a table near the door, where the two women were seated.

"Christ," Dex muttered. "That had me worried for a second."

"The way she's looking at you, I think she'll manage to let you know if she's going to bail," Malone said. "Though if she were my woman I'd probably stick a little closer, if you know what I mean." The old man grinned and Dex felt his face flush.

"Probably a good idea," he said and walked over to the table.

• • •

"...but I never expected to see him look so, I don't know..." Annabelle was saying as Dex approached the table.

"'Haggard' is the word that came to my mind when I saw him," the captain said, sipping some kind of tall cocktail.

"Hey now," Dex said, "I don't look that bad. I took a shower and everything." He grinned at the women and pulled up a seat.

"Not you," Annabelle said, seriously. "Pat Malone. He looks like hell. I can't even remember seeing anyone look like that. You?" she asked Zahara Zhang. The captain shook her head, long dark curls bouncing over her slim shoulders.

"Well, it's been a while," Dex said, "but back when I was living as a free man there were plenty of old people around. Most of them were throwbacks or nature freaks, who only ate food they grew themselves or whatever. It was kind of scary — guys who were less than my age now looking a hell of a lot worse than Malone, let me tell you. Wrinkles, white hair, thin skin, the whole death's door routine."

"Malone's no anti-tech freak," Annabelle said. "This isn't like that."

"Yeah, I've seen folks like Malone, too," Dex said. "They're just so damn old that the supplements don't cut it any more. It only lasts so long, they say. How old is he, anyway?"

"His personnel file says he's a hundred and twenty-seven," the captain said.

"Sounds about right," Dex said, sadly. "Even the expensive DNA-tailored supplements and tonics only give you a hundred and fifty tops. And I'm guessing none of us has enough dough for that kind of regime."

"It's so sad," Annabelle said. "He's still so full of life. I can't believe he's just going to decay until he dies. In this day and age you'd think we could come up with a better way."

"It used to be a lot worse," the captain said. "We've got it good in comparison to people just a hundred years ago."

"Sure," Annabelle said. "It still just seems wrong that you're perfectly fine one day, then you wake up the next morning and you're old." The three of them sat in silence with their thoughts, sipping their drinks. Their melancholy reverie was broken when a tall, blonde woman came over to their table.

"Anyone mind if I borrow Mr. Dexter here for a moment?" Melissa Vonruden said, flashing a wide smile. Annabelle shot a glance over to Dex, but he didn't seem to notice it.

"I'll be back in a minute," he said, rising from the table. As he turned away with Vonruden, he didn't see Annabelle's smouldering eyes on his back.

• • •

"Eduardo tells me you want to know about Stimsticks," she said, as she led them to a dark corner in the interior of the bar. Dex brought her up to speed on the similarities between Hazel and Harker's deaths and the information he'd learned about physical neurostimulators.

"Well, here's what I can tell you," Vonruden said, taking a long pull on her beer. "Joybuzzers and Stimsticks are the same thing. Slightly different packaging, different markets, but they function exactly the same way. Both are user configurable, though Stimsticks offer more options out of the box. If the user knows what they are doing, though, both units are easy to open up and adjust. They both deliver any kind of neurostim available from a node implant."

"I've only got the basic stim implant," Dex said. "What's a guy like me going to get out of one of those contraptions?"

"Well," Vonruden said, "your basic implant isn't going to get much out of a 'buzzer or Stimstick. The basic node just recreates a half dozen light intoxicants from online stims and mild pleasure plus the stunner reaction from a Stimstick. A decent upgrade, though, would simulate virtually anything from an online jolt, plus a very wide range of physical sensations."

"So, Harker and Hazel would have had to have upgraded nodes in order to get the goodies from the Stimstick, right?"

"Right," Vonruden said.

"But you can't tell by looking at person's nodes what each one is for," Dex said, "they all look pretty much the same."

"That's true," Vonruden said.

"So how would our killer know that the Stimstick was going to work?" Dex asked.

"Maybe he works in an upgrade salon?" Vonruden suggested.

"Maybe," Dex said. "What about a stim joint? Everyone who works there must have upgraded nodes."

"Sure," Vonruden said. "Hell, everyone who comes in the door would have them; nothing we sell would be any good without an upgrade. Same for the stim joints in M City."

"Huh," Dex grunted. He slapped Vonruden on the back and said, "Well, that's twice in a week I owe you a drink. You've just given me the first real lead in this mess. Why don't I get started on repaying you what I owe?" He left his hand on her shoulder as the two walked toward the bar.

From the table by the door, Annabelle watched as Dex bought the tall, beautiful, confident and very physically present Melissa Vonruden a drink.

Chapter Twenty-Four

ANNABELLE DIDN'T REMEMBER leaving the pub, or how she got back to the Red Fish Inn. She did remember the feeling of vertigo as she watched Dex with that woman from the goon squad. She remembered feeling like the walls of that horrible place were closing in on her and she remembered thinking she was going to lose consciousness. She must have found her way out of the bar then, found a train and made her way back to the guest house. She must have, because that's where she was now.

Though that wasn't entirely accurate. Her body was safely in her room at the Red Fish Inn, but she was really on her way to The Hot Spot, a stim bar in Marionette City. She hadn't been there since she started spending time with Dex; he didn't like stims and she was usually just fine with the stuff they served at Monte's. But she felt like hell and needed something to make that feeling go away. She needed something special and The Hot Spot was the place for something special.

The place was as crowded as she remembered it being. She liked that, it made her feel safe. She was alone but not alone, which was the best way to be when you needed to get happy. She pinged the bar for a list of the cocktails on offer and carefully pored over the menu. There were plenty of new items available since she had last visited, but she wasn't in an experimental mood. She wanted an old standby, a feeling that was as comfortable in its familiarity as it was in its chemical effects. She ordered a mixture they called Cranberry Sky, which was a cocktail made primarily of tranquilizers and endorphins.

What appeared to be a martini glass filled with a light pink liquid took a moment to materialize in her hand, but she felt the hit as soon as her order was in — her body instantly felt like it was made of rubber; even her lungs seemed to be soft and spongy. Slowly, riding the wave of comfort which seemed to roll over her body, came a feeling of contentment. It was as if all of a sudden, everything was right with the world and Annabelle wondered how she could ever have felt awkward, jealous or unhappy. She smiled and found a spot for her avatar at one of the small tables around The Hot Spot.

She sat, slowly sipping the drink, her avatar's action controlling the rate the neurostim mixture entered her system. She watched the other customers at the bar, mostly a sedate crowd this evening, mainly clustered together in groups of two or three, but many like her, alone at a table or at the bar, sipping whatever made them happy. Annabelle was about halfway through her drink and feeling fabulous, when a man stopped by her table.

"Mind if I join you," he asked. Annabelle looked and the man's avatar was totally bland. Most of the people in the bar had custom bodies, with fancy clothes and accessories. This fellow was strictly off the rack, but Annabelle was no snob. She knew plenty of people who had no interest in the aesthetics of the virtual world and she respected their opinion.

"Go ahead," she answered, gesturing to an empty chair across from her.

"So, what brings you out tonight?" he asked after he'd sat down and started sipping a drink of his own.

Annabelle thought. She remembered being so uncomfortable at the pub out there, unhappy with Dex for leaving her alone and going off with that woman. But she didn't feel any of those things any more and it all seemed a little ridiculous, now. "Just felt like time for a little splurge, you know," she said, her voice slow and sensuous. "Sometimes you just need to get out and get away from it all, don't you think"

"Definitely," the man said. "I feel like that a lot."

Annabelle noticed that he was paying her a lot of attention, but she didn't mind. It was nice to be noticed, nice to be admired, here where she felt like she truly belonged. Out there, she just felt wrong, like the body she wore wasn't really hers. She had always felt that way, then after meeting Dex she decided to finally do something about it. She had her physical body remade into the image of herself she saw in her mind, the version of herself she had made here, in M City.

She had hoped it would make things better and to a certain extent it did. When she looked in a mirror she now saw herself, not some stranger's eyes staring back at her. But, there was so much more to it than the way she looked. Regardless of the body she wore, she still felt like a freak out there. And the worst part of it all was that she so desperately wanted to feel comfortable out there now. Not for herself, but for Dex. Because she knew that the way she felt out there was exactly how he felt in here.

"So," she asked the man across from her, "what is it you want to get away from?"

"Oh, you know," he said, noncommittally, "the workaday world, I guess. Bosses, roommates, the whole treadmill."

"Isn't that right," Annabelle said, more for something to say than because she agreed with him. Even with all its complications, she liked her life. Even her problems were the good kind to have; making a hard relationship work with someone who is working just as hard to make it happen. She was lucky, she knew, and all of a sudden felt terrible about running out on Dex.

Something must have shown on her face, because the man

across from her said, "You okay? You look like you just got a shot of melancholy™ in there." He pointed at her glass.

"It's all right," Annabelle said. "I just think I made a really bad decision a little while back. I should probably go and do something about it."

"That seems like a good choice," the man said. "Choices are important. We don't get to make very many of them in this life, so it's important to make the right ones." His eyes bored into her and Annabelle got the strong impression he was trying to decide something about her. On the other hand, it might have just been the default expression on his bargain basement avatar.

"It's been nice talking to you," she said, as she drained the remains of her drink, "but I think I need to be going now. You have a good night, now." Annabelle stood, smiled at the man and linked out of The Hot Spot.

• • •

The man sipped his drink and made his choice.

CHAPTER TWENTY-FIVE

DEX DIDN'T KNOW how long he'd been talking to Melissa Vonruden when a couple of other people he knew from his time on the goon squad turned up. He hadn't seen either Buster Takahasi or Jay Shiraishi in the flesh since he'd left the street, but neither of them had changed much in the intervening years. By the time they turned up, Dex was on to his fourth pint and was feeling as gregarious as he got. He even was wishing he'd brought his cheap mandolin to the pub.

He got to talking with Buster and Shiraishi and it must have been a couple of hours before he noticed this bad feeling in the back of his mind. Annabelle. She couldn't possibly still be in the bar; the place was wall to wall with bodies now. He excused himself from his spot by the bar and started to weave his way through the pub grid-style, asking everyone he recognized when they'd last seen Annabelle. Half the crowd couldn't remember seeing her at all and those who had seen her were among the few early birds. Finally he found Zahara Zhang at a table in a far corner and she told him that she thought she saw Annabelle leave a few hours back.

"I think it was while you were talking to Vonruden," she said. "She didn't look too happy about it, either. I didn't think she was the jealous type, but you never know with people, do you."

"Oh, shit," Dex said for the second time that night. Only this time he knew he had fucked it up and Annabelle really had left. All because he was on to something on this case. He should have known better. It could have waited a day, or he could have talked to Vonruden with Annabelle there. He had promised to take care of her and at the first sniff of a lead, he'd abandoned her. He was an asshole and now he'd gone and ruined the best thing that had happened to him in decades. He sat at a small table and put his head in his hands.

• • •

Time stopped, it seemed. No one came over to see what was wrong and Dex didn't want them to. He didn't know what he could do to fix this. He was too scared to even ping Annabelle, because he didn't want to find out that she was blocking him. Between the beers, his overactive imagination and the knowledge that it was all his fault, he had worked himself into a solid state of despair, when he felt a hand light on his shoulder.

"Go away," he said, without looking up.

"I tried that," a familiar voice said. "I don't think it was such a good idea." Dex looked up and saw Annabelle's face looking down at him, smiling sadly.

"I'm so sorry," he said, his voice cracking. "I never should have left you alone here. I don't know what I was thinking; please forgive me."

Annabelle sat down next to Dex and put her arm around him. "And I never should have left without telling you I was going. There, we're even."

"Not even close, kiddo," Dex said, turning to look at her. Their faces were so close that he could feel her breath hot on his skin. He tried not to think about it, tried not to think about what he would do if she were only different, only more like him. He didn't want to fuck it up again.

He nearly fell off the chair when he felt her lips on his, her mouth hot against his own. Time stopped again, until he heard a voice from what sounded like a million klicks away yell, "Get a room, you two," and raucous laughter from the bar. They pulled away from each other and Dex said, "I can't believe you just did that."

"Me either," Annabelle said, laughing. "Though, to be fair, I do have a lot of chemical help right now."

"You're doped up?" Dex asked.

"To the virtual eyeballs," Annabelle answered, smiling goofily.

"Well, let's hear it for better living though chemistry," Dex said and Annabelle laughed again. "You want to stay here or are you done for the night?" He didn't want to hope for anything, but he couldn't help himself.

"I figure I've got about three hours of joy juice in me," Annabelle said. "It's your call. You want to spend those hours here, I'm happy to tag along. If you'd rather go back to your apartment," she lowered her eyelids and looked him squarely in the face, "I'm happy to tag along there, too."

Dex blinked twice, then stood. Annabelle put her hand in his and together they walked over to Pat Malone and gave the man a quick salute. "Great party man and I wish you the best in your golden years. However, my lady and I have to make like a tree and get the hell out of here."

Malone clapped Dex on the back and said, "Good man." To Annabelle, he said, "You've got a keeper here, honey. But don't do anything you'll regret later, it will just make things harder in the long run."

"Thanks, Pat," she smiled at him and kissed him on the cheek. "For everything." Then she and Dex walked, hand in hand, out of the pub.

• • •

Two and a half hours later, Dex walked into the lav and ran the tap in the sink for a moment. He washed his face and looked in the mirror at his naked body. Nothing special there, he thought. Not like her. She was perfect, the pain and expense of the body moulding she'd endured had seen to that. But it was more than just the shape of her body, the feel of her skin — it was everything. For a couple of hours, he had been happier than he could ever remember being. But now Annabelle had left to go back to her hotel and she was going to be on an early flight the next morning back to Europa. He didn't know when, or if he would see her again.

Dex had never felt so confused — on one hand, he felt wonderful. Being with Annabelle, really together, was fantastic. It was the best thing he could ever have hoped for, it was so much more than he ever dreamed they would have together. But he also knew that when the chemicals wore off, she was still the same Annabelle who was terrified of the party, who could barely stand to give him a kiss. She hadn't changed, but things between them had.

Would it be worth it, he wondered, if this was the end with Annabelle? Would those few hours of joy be worth all the days he wouldn't have with her? He didn't know.

He left the lav and poured a shot of rum. He was still a little drunk from the party, but he didn't care. If he spent the whole next day in bed, that would postpone the talk he would have to have with Annabelle. And at that moment, anything that put off the inevitable was good with him. He slugged down the drink, feeling the burn down his throat and into his stomach. He knew this was nothing like what Annabelle felt when she was on stims, but he thought he understood how she managed to get over her fears for him. At that moment, he would do anything for her, but she was gone. He could only hope she wasn't gone forever.

CHAPTER TWENTY-SIX

THE MAN HELD two items in his hands. In his left hand, he held the knife. It had been his great-great-great grandmother's knife. He doubted that she had used it like he did, but he'd never met the woman. She died long before he was born. Back then people only lived a hundred years if they were very lucky or very rich. No one in his family had ever been either of those things. The man never knew exactly how he ended up with Grandma Burback's beautiful knife, or why she had such an object in the first place. He didn't think about it very much. It didn't matter how you got somewhere, what mattered is what you did when you were there.

In his right hand, the man held his new, calibrated Joybuzzer. He had tried and tried with different settings, even hurting himself a few times, but he finally got it right. He was pretty sure that now it would make them feel the way he wanted them to feel; strong enough that they would be compliant and let him do his work, but not so strong that it became about them. The work was not about the candidates, not at all. It was about him. Him and his choices.

He was feeling good. Gerry was out somewhere again and the man was alone in the apartment. He sat on his bed, weighing the two objects in his hands. The knife was so much heavier than the modern contraption, which he felt was appropriate somehow. The 'buzzer was just a tool, after all. It was replaceable and while the man strongly preferred the work when the candidates were buzzed up and happy, it was not strictly necessary. The knife, on the other hand, was as integral to the work as he was himself. He often thought of the knife as his partner. They were a team. He was the one who chose and then the knife did the work.

And he had chosen again. She would be an excellent candidate, he thought. She seemed to understand about the power of choices. It was almost as if she were telling him that she would be a good candidate. Yes, she would be pleased to help him make the choice. He was looking forward to this one. After the last one, which was so unsatisfying, he wanted to make a good choice. He would start looking for her right away. The one who called herself Annabelle Lewis. The man decided that she would die next.

CHAPTER TWENTY-SEVEN

DEX HAD HAD worse hangovers. But he hadn't felt much worse in his life. The combination of pounding head, roiling stomach and aching heart were doing a number on him. He doubted that any amount of Flying Fish Tonix would make a dent in how terrible he felt, but he swigged down a good measure just in case. He didn't bother to check the time, or have the apartment un-dim the windows. Morning, afternoon, what did it matter? He felt like hell and knew that he deserved it.

What kind of a man was he? Taking advantage of Annabelle when she was high as the sky on who knew what kind of crazy brain chemical. How could he have let her think that he needed her embodied self so badly that she had to do that to herself? And then to go merrily along with her crazy, drug fuelled plan? He felt sick and he was sure it wasn't just from the booze.

Thankfully, she would be out of the city by now, so he wouldn't have to fear that she would just show up at the apartment. He didn't want to talk to her, not yet, so he was staying offline. He knew that wouldn't last — tomorrow he had to go back to that pit of depression, Barrett and Brar, and he'd need to go online then. Maybe he just wouldn't go in. Maybe he'd just quit. He had looked over his cash flow the other day and was surprised to find that he spent quite a bit less than he brought in. In fact, he spent less than he earned from his work with the Cubicle Men alone. It certainly made giving the two finger salute to B&B look pretty attractive.

He knew that he was just avoiding thinking about Annabelle, but fantasizing about quitting work was better than worrying about how much he'd damaged his relationship with her, so he stayed aboard that train of thought. He had quite a lot of cash saved up, so he could afford to have to pay for his own apartment. He wouldn't get anything nicer than his current place, but that was the same as it would be if he just stayed where he was. He guessed that he was just frugal by nature, because he'd always thought that banking the extra cash was better than spending it on something frivolous. That seven year old rum, for example. When he looked at things clearly, he could certainly afford to give up the security and benefits of B&B, but it would eat into his savings and he didn't like that.

On the other hand, not having to go in to some vile office park every day and endure the bullshit from underworked overpaid middle managers and, even worse, the suck ups like Mister Mouse — now that was maybe something worth spending some cash on. If he lost his income from B&B and had the expense of his own housing, that would seriously make a dent in his savings, though, and then flying over to see Annabelle would be— Damn it, Dex thought. I don't want to think about her now.

He'd been doing all this pondering while still in bed and he finally got up. The room was only spinning very sightly, which he took to be a good sign. He walked into the lav, showered and dressed, then wandered over to his box of food bricks. His stomach flipped a little, but he steeled himself and opened up a bar. He took a nibble and waited to make sure it stayed in place, then ate another bite. It wasn't long before his head and stomach seemed almost normal, but he still felt like shit.

Work, he thought. Work was the answer. He had a lot to look at on the Hazel case and the sooner he got on it the sooner he could catch the sick fuck who was behind the killings. He stretched, cracking his neck, and after pulling a large glass of water, he got comfortable and logged in to the Cubicle Men's system.

He checked his messages, saw that there was one from Pat Malone thanking everyone for the party and one from Melissa Vonruden. Dex opened Vonruden's message and read it.

"After our talk, I took a look at the case file on Harker and Ramer. I noticed that the physical evidence of neurostimulation on Ramer was quite different from that found in Harker's system. I ran a scan on it, to see if I could get the specific patterns and match it to something I've seen before. It was totally off the scale. There is nothing on the market which can even be DIY'd into something that could give that kind of jolt. However, there are rumours of new 'buzzer models coming out. Maybe there's something I just don't know about out there. Sorry I couldn't be more help. —MV"

Dex was disappointed that Vonruden hadn't turned up anything more concrete, but he couldn't make evidence out of nothing. So he just flagged the message to the case file and then started going through the automated search responses from his queries.

He couldn't see anything useful from his request for information about steel blades. There was the usual history and composition data, which he ignored. There were boards for collectors of the things, but they were all full of information about trading the items or maintaining them. He found one link to a woman who was making the things, but she was located in Afrika. It gave Dex a thought, though, and he ran a request for an analysis of the steel fragments found in both Harker and Hazel's bodies, to see if the blade could be aged. If it turned out to be a recently made item, he might be able to trace the killer that way. If it was old, though, he didn't think he'd have a hope.

As opposed to the feeling he got when he saw the cross reference results for people who had purchased either a Joybuzzer or

Stimstick and a set of Hold-Alls wrist restraints. There were hundreds of names on the list, but when he drilled down to show only the people who lived, worked or traveled to the city, he got it down to a list of only forty-eight. It was plenty of names, but he knew that with time he could find out if any of those people were in the areas where Harker or Hazel were killed at the times of their deaths. Rather, he knew Annabelle could do it. The thought made his stomach clench up again.

He knew she would help him, regardless of whatever came of the previous night. She was a professional and he knew that this case bothered her almost as much as it bothered him. But he also knew that he couldn't ask her to help with the case without talking to her about other things. And he just wasn't ready for that. He knew he couldn't delay forever, but he could put it off for now. So he moved on to the next report.

As soon as Dex paged over to the file, he felt his stomach drop. Four. There had been four other killings which fit the same evidence as Harker's and Hazel's deaths. Three men and a woman had been found dead in abandoned buildings in brown sector over the last six months. Each had been cut with a steel blade, each had been bound with polymer rope and each had neurostimulants in their systems. The two earliest victims didn't fit the pattern exactly — both had traces of synthetic neurostims rather than naturally occurring neurochemicals; and the second victim, the woman, had been severely beaten before she died. The two later victims, though, might have been blueprints for Luis Harker's murder. The evidence was identical. Dex wondered why the pattern hadn't been noticed before now.

He looked at the victims' files and saw that two of the male victims were not employed, at least not in a conventional job and were well known to be active in the intense stimulation scene. No one was missing them, no one paid for their deaths to be investigated and it was easy to chalk their deaths up to stimulation play gone wrong. The beaten woman was a middle manager at one of the firms and their Security had looked into her disappearance and eventual death. They discovered that she'd had a gambling habit and assuming that her death was related to debts, they had dropped the investigation. The fourth victim's death had been only perfunctorily investigated by his employer's Security team, then dropped without any conclusions being drawn. No one had realized that the deaths were related, because no one agency had investigated more than their one area of interest. It was typical, Dex thought, angrily.

He added the information from the other deaths into his composite case file and requested the neuro scans from the two victims whose deaths had been investigated. He didn't expect much, especially from the Security files on the man's death. But he had to see if there was anything on the files which could help him find the killer. He knew the killer had struck at least six times — six times in as many months. And Luis Harker's death had occurred within a few weeks of Hazel's murder, so it appeared that the killer's pace was increasing. It had been a week since Hazel had been killed. Was the killer preparing to strike again?

Dex was finishing up his request for access to the files from the two corporate Security teams, when his system pinged. He was so embroiled in the work that he had forgotten everything else that had occurred in the last twenty-four hours and he automatically answered. Of course, it was Annabelle.

CHAPTER TWENTY-EIGHT

"HOW WERE YOU feeling this morning?" Annabelle asked. Dex felt his heart pounding so loud that he could hear the blood in his ears. He felt a little bit like he was going to lose consciousness. He fought to keep control.

"Not so good," he answered. He didn't know what to say. "You made your flight okay?" he asked, wincing at the lameness of the question.

"No problem," Annabelle said. "I'm home now."

"Good," Dex said. "That's good," he repeated. There was an awkward pause as neither of them said anything.

"I've been working on the case..." Dex said, breaking the silence but not the tension.

"Good," Annabelle said, "did you find anything new?" Relieved to be on safer ground, Dex gave Annabelle a brief synopsis of what he'd found.

"Send me those names," she said, referring to the list of people who had bought both Hold-Alls and Stimsticks or Joybuzzers. "I can get a script together to look for matches on people who were in brown sector at the time Harker or Hazel was killed. It's going to take a while, though..." her voice trailed off.

"I know it will take time," Dex said. "And I'm not trying to rush you. But I am worried that the killer will strike again soon. I feel like we're close to something here and I don't even want to think about what it would be like if someone else dies while I was investigating."

"I know," Annabelle said. "I'm on it."

"Thanks," Dex said, letting out a breath he hadn't known he was holding.

"So..." Annabelle said.

"Yeah," Dex answered. "This is a bit awkward, isn't it?"

"Look," Annabelle said. "I don't want you to think that you did something wrong last night. I know you and I bet that you've got this image of me right now as this fragile thing you took advantage of when she was weak and doped up and that it somehow makes you the bad guy. And that's not even close to the truth. I'm a grown up, with a long and colourful history with fine neurochemical substances. I knew exactly what I was taking and what would happen to me. And I knew exactly what I was doing with you, too. You don't have to feel responsible for anything other than yourself."

"Jeez, Annabelle," Dex said, "am I really that predictable? And pathetic?"

She laughed, but it wasn't with a lot of mirth. "I think after all this time I've got you figured out, mister," she said. "And I don't think you're pathetic, it's just the unfortunate flip side of that wonderful chivalry I love about you."

Dex grunted. "Well, at least you're still saying nice things about me," he said, "so I guess that means we're still on speaking terms."

"Of course, we're still on speaking terms, you fool," Annabelle said. "What happened was — well, it was strange and not at all what I planned or expected, but I don't think we've completely fucked things up. Not at all. It would take a lot to make me give you up. Don't forget, I liked you for a very long time before you'd even give me the time of day." She paused and her voice grew serious again. "But I don't think I really realized until now that the you I thought I liked wasn't who you really are."

"And," Dex asked expectantly, "what about that guy? Do you like him?"

"I do," Annabelle said softly. "I still like you, Dex, I still like you a lot. It's just hard." Dex heard her sigh. "You're not exactly the man I dreamed of being with."

Dex said nothing for a moment. Then, he answered, "Neither are you."

Silence. Then Annabelle said, "Okay then. So what about that? You know where I stand, but what about you? Have things changed for you, now?"

"No," Dex said. "Yes... I don't know. Damn it, Annabelle, I can't imagine my life without you any more. These last months have been better than anything I can remember, even with everything being so — tough. But last night..." His voice trailed off. "This is it," he said, finally. "Cards on the table time; no bullshit."

"No bullshit," Annabelle agreed, all the lightness and laughter gone from her voice.

"This morning, when I thought I'd ruined everything between us, I asked myself if it was worth it; if one night with you, here in the physical world, was worth never being with you again."

"And?"

"And I hate myself for it," Dex said, "but it was."

Annabelle said nothing for a long time. Finally she said, "I think that's really a compliment," she said, "but it doesn't feel like it, somehow."

"I'm sorry," Dex said, his voice a croak.

Annabelle said, "It's okay, I get it." She quoted, "'Tis better to have loved and lost...'"

"It doesn't feel better," Dex said, miserably.

"But I'm not lost, either," Annabelle said. "Look, I can't say that what happened last night is going to happen all the time — hell, I can't say that it's going to ever happen again. At the moment I still

can't really believe it happened at all. But it does prove one thing —
the gulf between us is both larger and smaller than we thought."

"So, you're not giving me the boot?" Dex asked.

"You aren't getting rid of me that easily, Mr. Dexter," Annabelle
said, the sly twist back in her voice. Dex was happy to hear the
sound again. "Not after all the work I put in to get you. Now, I'd
better get going on that script for you. There are way more important things for us to be doing than agonizing over doing something
we both wanted to do, that was plenty enjoyable at the time. Neither of us has been thirty in a lot of years — we have no excuse for
that kind of drama."

Dex laughed and felt something almost physical in his chest
break open. It was relief, a pure release of the tension he'd been
feeling trapped by all day. How he ever thought Annabelle could
hate him, he now couldn't understand. She was the most forgiving,
most patient person he had ever known. And she could make him
laugh, always, no matter how grim the circumstances. He couldn't
imagine what he wouldn't do for her.

"Right," he said. "Let's get to work."

CHAPTER TWENTY-NINE

IN SPITE OF all his wild plans, Dex did go in to work at B&B the next day as normal. The thoughts of quitting, just walking out the door and never looking back, were still there, but they had moved to the back of his mind again. Like most crazy ideas that go against the grain of what everybody does, they sat in the corner and stewed, but Dex stopped thinking about them seriously. Most of the time.

Annabelle's script was grinding away at the list of names Dex had given her, but it was slow going. She'd had to find a way to automate her unauthorized access to the master files on everywherenet which tracked people's movements in the physical world. She claimed that it wasn't particularly difficult, it just meant that each name had to be researched separately, which took time. By the end of the first day, her script had processed almost ten people — none of which had been anywhere near the victims. At the rate it was progressing, she would be finished the list in about a week. Dex just hoped it would be soon enough to stop the killer before someone else was killed.

Dex felt like he was out of leads. His investigation of the steel fragments revealed that the blade used to kill Hazel and Harker was the same one, which was good evidence, but it didn't tell Dex anything he didn't already know. It also showed that the blade was old, quite old, made at least a few hundred years previously. It would be impossible to trace.

Dex had nothing to do. He always hated this part of an investigation, when there's nothing to do but wait to see if the trail you've been chasing ends up somewhere. In this case, the waiting was worse than usual. Dex feared that every second he spent waiting was one step closer to another murder.

• • •

A couple of days into the work week, Dex's personal system pinged near the end of the day. Assuming it was Annabelle, he answered without looking. It was Pat Malone instead.

"Pat," Dex said. "Good to hear from you again. How is retirement treating you?"

"Like a bastard treats his worst enemy," Malone answered, gruffly. "I've never been so bored in my life."

"Catching up on the latest vids isn't doing it for you?" Dex asked.

"For christ's sakes," Malone barked, "I'm not dead yet — I've got to have something to do with my mind. Good thing I talked Zizou into letting me keep my access to the case files, you know just for reading material in my declining years. I've been following your case — it looks like a humdinger."

"And then some," Dex agreed. "And there's only one lead and it's taking forever to run it down. I kind of feel like I can relate to your conundrum — there's plenty going on but nothing to do."

"Well, if you're looking for a way to kill a couple of hours, how about you join me for a beer at the Sprocket tonight? You work day shifts, right?"

"Yeah," Dex said. "I don't have anything going on tonight. Sure, I'll meet you there."

"Name your time," Malone said. "I've got nothing filling my calendar, believe me." They set a date for seven-thirty and ended the call. Dex wondered if Malone really was just lonely and bored or if there was more to it than that. The old man was far from senile and over the years he'd been a shining star on the goon squad. Dex knew that it took more than muscle and jive to stay tops on the streets for that long.

• • •

Annabelle called Dex later that day, while he was on the train to green sector to meet Malone. He filled her in on his call from the former lieutenant and she updated Dex on her everywherenet script.

"I'm about halfway done," she said and Dex groaned. "I know, I know," she said, "It's painfully slow. But we've eliminated twenty-three people already and that's good, isn't it?"

"No matches," Dex said, thoughtfully.

"There was one person who had been in brown sector several times in the last six months," Annabelle said, "but when I looked at the logs closer she was always going to the same building, staying a half hour, then leaving again. The building isn't one of the kill sites. I checked around and it looks like a stimplay place."

"A what?" Dex asked.

"You can be so naive," Annabelle said, laughing. "It's a place where people go to get whacked out on stims and then do stuff to each other. Whips and chains kind of thing, usually, but there's a whole shopping list of sensations for sale." She giggled evilly. "I can send you an address, if you want to check it out."

"Oh, stop it," Dex said, feeling his face get hot. "You know that's not me."

"Yeah, I know" Annabelle said, laughing. "I do love winding you up, though."

"And you do a fine job, kiddo, that you do."

"Hey, speaking of sins of the flesh," Annabelle said, "are we still on for dinner and whatever in a couple of days?"

"You bet," Dex said. "I'll see you at Monte's at 0300 UTC?"

"Sounds good," Annabelle said and her voice made Dex smile. It was almost back to normal between them, though they'd only spoken via voice calls since the weekend. This would be their first face to face meeting since the weekend and Dex was nervous. Even if it was only M City.

• • •

He was just finishing up his call with Annabelle when he reached the heavy glass door leading in to The Cog and Sprocket. Dex pushed it open and while the place was nowhere near as full as it had been for Malone's party, the wall of sound that hit him as he walked over the threshold was intense. So many people, in such a small space, make an awful lot of noise.

Dex pushed his way into the bar and found Pat Malone on what Dex now thought of as the man's usual stool near the middle of the long bar. He perched on a free seat next to Malone and signalled the barman for a pint. "Am I glad to see you," Malone said while Dex waited for his beer.

"It's good to see you, too, Pat," Dex said, trying not to stare. He had been the worse for wear when he'd left the bar the night of the party, but he surely remembered what Malone looked like. The man had visibly aged in the few days that had passed. The wrinkles around his mouth and eyes had etched more deeply and a whole swarm of new ones had appeared on his face. His skin seemed to be becoming thinner and more translucent and his hair was now completely white. It was like looking at an ancient ancestor, rather than the man himself.

"I know," Malone said, reading Dex's expression, "I'm a scarier looking brute now than I ever was back in my nose breaking days." Malone took a long pull on his beer, while looking at his reflection in the mirror behind the bar. "Getting old is shit, Dex. I don't even know how much time I have left. Probably a couple of weeks."

"Christ, man," Dex said. "How can it be so fast?"

"That's the price of long life," Malone said, ruefully. "When the magic stops working, it's a fast ride downhill on a speeding train." He took another sip of the amber brew. "Maybe it's for the best. I can't imagine years of this fucking half life," he gestured with his half empty glass. "Retirement — ha! I honestly would rather be dead than have to do nothing for years."

"I'm sorry," Dex said, lamely.

"No," Malone said, his voice taking on a tone of forced cheerfulness, "I'm sorry. I didn't ask you down here to listen to me bitch and moan; I asked you down here to cheer me up. So, there's two topics of conversation bound to get me out of this self-pitying wallow I've gotten myself into — your nasty poseur sushi chef murderer and that sweet thing you were glued to last time I saw you. You pick which one you start with."

"What's a sushi chef?" Dex asked.

Malone laughed, a big guffaw straight from the gut. "You young people," he said. "Never mind, it's before your time. Anyway, give me the goods."

"I've got nothing," Dex said, miserably. "You've read the case file, right?" Malone nodded. "Well, that's pretty much all there is. I've got a list of all the people who bought one of those Stimstick things and who also bought the kind of wrist restraints that were used on Harker and Hazel. Annabelle's cross referencing everyone on that list to see if they were in brown sector at the time of the murders. It's taking forever, though, and she's gotten absolutely no hits so far. I'm starting to feel like it's going to be a dead end and then I'm fresh out of ideas."

"Hmm," the old man thought for a moment. "Did you check to see if you can trace the knife?"

"Yeah," Dex said. "It's old. A couple of centuries — like maybe from your era," he added, grinning.

"Very good," Malone said, laughing again. "We're even for the sushi joke then, junior. So no joy from the blade. What's Annabelle's project again? Cross referencing what?"

Dex explained about the use of Hold-Alls and either Joybuzzers or Stimsticks in the murders and what he was getting Annabelle to do. "Hrm," Malone grunted. "Pretty clever. What about that note I saw from Vonruden? The Ramer case was different somehow, wasn't it."

"Yeah," Dex said. "It looks like some kind of homebrew upgrade was done on the Stimstick. The levels of neurostims were through the roof."

"I thought I saw something else in there," Malone said. "Mind if I take another look?"

"Please," Dex said. "I'll take all the help I can get." He watched as Malone's eyes took on the glassy stare of someone going online. Less than a minute later, Malone was refocussing on the bar and his mouth was twitching into a smile.

"You're going to have to buy me a beer, junior," Malone said, grinning now. "I think I maybe just found you another lead."

CHAPTER THIRTY

"IT WASN'T A homebrew upgrade," Malone said, lifting his newly refilled glass to his lips.

"What?"

"Vonruden, who knows her stuff in this area, let me tell you, said that neither 'buzzers nor Stimsticks can deliver the punch Ramer got," Malone said. "Not with any amount of screwing and soldering. It had to be something else, something she'd never seen before."

"Well, if Vonruden doesn't know what it is," Dex said, "what the hell could it be?"

"Totally homemade, from scratch," Malone speculated. "Or a new product that isn't on the market yet."

"Right," Dex said, getting excited. "A prototype. They do that all the time at B&B. When a new thing comes up, employees get first crack at the can. Customer Service and Sales need to know what the product does, the gung ho types can start the buzz machine and if there's a problem, we're cheap and easy guinea pigs."

"Vonruden's note mentioned that the word on the street is that the outfit that makes Joybuzzers, Tractor or something, is coming up with something new soon," Malone said.

"No, not Tractor," Dex said. "I bet it's Gractor. I know them; they are competitors in my employer's market. They make good stuff, actually. I have a few Gractor nodes myself."

"Well, you and your killer might have something in common, then," Malone said. "And now that I've given you a new lead, you can give me all the gory details about you and sweet Annabelle Lewis."

• • •

Dex didn't want to talk about his bizarre relationship, but if dead men tell no tales then almost dead men don't tell that many. And he knew he could use some advice, since he couldn't trust his own judgment any more.

"So, Annabelle told me that you helped her out when she first joined the organization," Dex began.

"You better get to the good stuff soon, son," Malone said, a twinkle in his eye. "Sure, I greased a few wheels for her, but it's debatable that I needed to. She's one in a million that one."

"You don't have to tell me," Dex said. "But then you know about her, how shall I put it, locational preferences?"

"I know she's freaked out by the physical world and only lives online," Malone said. "Or at least, that was what I thought she was like. Recent events seem to belie that assumption."

"Yeah, recent events," Dex muttered. "No, that's Annabelle, all right. The trouble is that I'm the exact opposite. I'm okay being in there, obviously. But it's totally fake to me. And relationships — well, I don't exactly have a stellar track record, but I've always known one thing: it's all about the real world for me. I've never cared much about the details of the body, but there's got to be one, if you know what I mean."

"Yeah," Malone said, kindly. "I know exactly what you mean. So how did this thing with Annabelle ever even get started? It sounds like you just shouldn't be into each other from the start."

"You know how it is," Dex said, ordering another beer when the barman passed by. "We knew each other from the squad and for some reason she took a shine to me. She didn't know about my...

tastes at the time, but I always blew her off, anyway. And that's how it was. But then, we were working together on this case and one thing led to another..."

"And you fell for her," Malone said.

"Yeah," Dex said. "It's been hell on both of us. She's tried harder than I have, though; that's obvious after last weekend."

"It looked to me like she was doing more than just trying," Malone said, his eyebrows waggling.

"Yeah, well," Dex said, "it wasn't all flowers and kisses, I'm afraid."

"You didn't fuck it all up, did you?" Malone asked, glowering at Dex.

"Miraculously, no," Dex said. "But... it's complicated."

"For christ's sake, boy," Malone exploded, "it's always god-damned complicated. If love were easy we'd all be pie eyed and gooey the whole damn time. It sounds to me like you've got yourself someone who wants you bad enough to change her whole life for you. And you're sitting here with this old decrepit bastard, when you could be taking her for a ride to the moon. What kind of an idiot are you, anyway?"

"The kind of idiot you called and invited down here, asshole," Dex shot back.

Malone laughed his big belly laugh and slapped Dex on the back. "Right you are, junior, right you are. Well, then, let's not waste our time here, shall we. Let's get ourselves good and shitfaced, then tomorrow you can go and give that wonderful woman who is way too good for the likes of you a little of what she gave you last week-end."

"What the hell are you talking about?" Dex said, confused and embarrassed.

"Who cares if it feels like a cardboard box to you?" Malone said. "If she wants to be together in M City, then make it happen. Trust me. If you really care about her, making her happy will have an amazingly similar effect on you, even if what you're doing isn't exactly your thing."

"You sound very certain," Dex said.

"Oh, I am, son," Malone said. "I wasn't always this lonely old man you see before you, lost in a pint of very fine expensive ale. I once had a great love of my own, you know. And he liked opera. I will still, for the life of me, never understand why. But he ate that shit up. So I sat through it and not just online either, where I could turn off the sound and do something else. Oh, no, this was back when there were real theatres and everything out here. And we would go once or twice a year and my ass would go numb and he would be glowing he was so happy. And goddamn it," Malone said, staring off into the mirror, "so would I."

The two men said nothing for a while, each of them sipping their beers. Finally, Dex broke the silence. "What happened?" he asked.

"What happened when?" Malone asked.

"To your man," Dex said. "What happened to him?"

"Same thing that's happening to me," Malone said bitterly. "About a decade ago."

"I'm sorry," Dex said.

"So am I, junior," Malone said. "So am I."

CHAPTER THIRTY-ONE

DEX FELT LIKE someone had taken a pair of extra capacity disk nodes and screwed them right into his eyeballs. Just blinking hurt. And his head pounded. And his stomach felt like a very excitable octopus was living in it. That Pat Malone was a bad influence, he thought.

A half bottle of FlyingFish later, about a quarter of which finally stayed down and Dex was ready to face another day at Barrett and Brar. He had other goals than just making it through another workday. Between client calls and inane internal reports, he was going to be snooping on the competition. Gractor.

Dex knew about the node implants that Gractor made — they were mostly for the same purposes as the ones that B&B made. Among the more popular ones were those for neurostims, of course, but they also made disk nodes, video and audio recorders, network speed upgrades, and physical stimulators for online interaction.

Companies like Gractor and B&B were huge; everyone who used a neural connection to everywherenet needed at least a couple of node implants. Even guys like Dex, who was pretty meat and potatoes when it came to the interface, wore more than the basic package. And of course, the upgrade treadmill was the real money maker for them — as the network expanded and more and more could be done online, people wanted better connections and a more robust experience. It kept Dex and his co-workers employed and it kept the shareholders of Gractor and B&B in luxury.

Dex knew B&B's product line inside out and backwards, but he only had a consumer's knowledge of Gractor's offerings. So, while he was helping a new customer adjust a new taste simulator node, Dex electronically snuck out of the office. He went online and found the full listing of Gractor's products. He skimmed past the nodes and found an entire section of completely different items. The company's full name was Gractor Devices and Dex had assumed the second word was just a remnant of an earlier era. Instead, it turned out that Gractor still made devices. And rather a lot of them.

Dex quickly scanned the list of typical consumer products: implantable viewscreens, food brick processors, fabric shapers, pigment applicators — the usual. Then he got to the section of more niche products, which included Joybuzzers. He found the marketing page about them and read the hype carefully. As he had seen before, the marketing spiel was heavily weighted toward the pleasure creating aspect of the products. But even then, the technical details made it clear that the 'buzzers were easily user configurable to deliver a 'wide variety of 100% safe physical stimulation, unattainable any other way.' Dex rolled his eyes and in the process caught a glimpse of some small print near the bottom. It was a Valued Customer login for more information.

Dex knew about that sort of thing. It was primarily for employees, so you could get access to your discount and the new products. At B&B at least, there were no outside Valued Customers at all. It was just a carrot the marketing folks dangled at repeat buyers. Dex didn't have the login credentials for Gractor's VC area, but that wasn't much of an impediment. The Cubicle Men's system would be able to get him in, just like it got him access to B&B's Security files on Hazel's death. He sent a request for the access, then paged over to the rest of Gractor's catalogue while he waited.

• • •

The corporate hand had fingers in a lot of pies, it seemed. They also made a series of non-lethal weapons targeted to the Security market — stunners, knuckledusters, disabling spray, the usual. Dex noticed with some considerable interest that they offered several comprehensive packages, each of which included a couple of weapons, an armour suit and restraints. He guessed that the idea was for a firm to simply order one of these packages for each of its Security members. It certainly made the procurement easy.

He opened the details for one of the packages and found what he had started to suspect — the restraints in the higher quality packages were Hold-Alls brand. Dex checked into it further and saw that it was a subsidiary of Gractor which manufactured the restraints, along with the body armour and other assorted Security related materials. Dex had no proof that the killer had even used a Joybuzzer brand tool, but it still seemed like too much of a coincidence to ignore.

Dex didn't like coincidences. He paged back over to his Cubicle Men account and waited impatiently for his Gractor VC access to come through. Staring at his message inbox wasn't helping anything, so Dex took a breath. He was between calls, so he got up and walked over to the break room. He poured a cup of brown water and sipped. He made a face and dumped it into the recyclatron. He was tired of drinking that swill. Tired of trying to sell people shit they didn't need and tired of putting up with co-workers spying on his every move in the hopes that they would catch him in some unapproved activity they could report.

He sighed and returned to his station. He caught Mister Mouse peeping at him from behind silvered lenses. For a moment he was just about to walk over there and give the annoying little man a shot to the nose, but instead he just sat in his chair and stared at the man. Dex did nothing for a full minute, simply looked at the other man. Mister Mouse looked away, of course, but couldn't help himself and kept glancing Dex's way. Eventually, he just got up and went to the lav. Dex laughed aloud, causing a half dozen other co-workers to glance his way. He didn't care.

He logged back into the Cubicle Men's system and saw that his access to Gractor's VC area had been opened. He entered the appropriate credentials in the system and was instantly rewarded. "Get the new Joybuzzer, now!" was emblazoned over the Valued Clients page in large font. "Five times the power, fifty times the pleasure†," the copy continued. "The most intense sensation product ever created is now in a device the size of your little finger. Works with Gractor SensationPlus nodes*. Available worldwide next quarter, but get a sneak preview now. Order one now; available for immediate delivery."

He jumped down to the small print and saw that the items were pretty much universally compatible with any brand of upgraded stim node. He looked at the output figures and even assuming that the numbers were inflated two or three times, this new 'buzzer was head and shoulders beyond the current model. It sounded an awful lot like what Hazel had been hit with, Dex thought.

Dex paged back to Gractor's corporate information. He knew that the killer had to live, work or travel regularly to the city, so he searched for any corporate presence in town. Finally it seemed like he was really making progress in the case. Gractor had a manufacturing facility right in the city, in gray sector.

Dex had the Cubicle Mens's automated system pull a full employee list for the facility and he sat back. He had the feeling that he was close now and it fired him up like nothing else in the world. He still had the niggling fear that it might be too late, that the killer would strike again before Dex could get to the bottom if it, but he felt better than he had since Hazel disappeared. Honestly, he felt better than he had in longer than he could remember.

He'd been thinking about Malone's words from the previous night all day and had come to a decision. He pulled up B&B's own Valued Clients area and scrolled through the virtual sensation nodes. He had only the basic implant which let him move through M City without falling over. He could feel virtual interactions, enough to hold a glass or shake hands, but it was pretty rudimentary. With an upgrade, he'd be able feel more, a lot more. He had never wanted to and even now he was vaguely disgusted by the prospect, but before he could change his mind, he hit the Buy Now button.

• • •

Ordinarily, he would have just chosen the automatic deductions from his pay to cover the cost of the upgrade, but Dex was having the feeling that he might not be an employee long enough to make the payments and he knew how much of a hassle the paperwork would be if he quit before the debt was done. So he just ponied up the cash for the upgrade and scheduled an implantation for when his shift ended. They had a salon on site which he knew did competent work, so Dex was fine with having them do the upgrade. Besides, he would need it for the next evening and he wanted to have tried it out at least once first.

After his workday was done, Dex shouldered his way into B&B's onsite salon. There was no one else getting any work done, so they had him in the chair almost as soon as he walked in the door.

"You want any stims before we start?" the pleasantly pudgy young woman operator asked. Dex shook his head and watched as she shrugged her shoulders. "You sure?" she asked. "The old one will probably hurt coming out."

"Just get it over with," Dex growled, having had second, third and fourth thoughts by now. She looked at him coldly and clamped a long, thin stainless tool on the node just under Dex's lower lip. It did hurt as the tool emitted an electrical pulse which would separate the two parts of the node as well as the connection to both his implanted silicon and his own nerves. It didn't take long, though, and when the node popped out Dex felt nothing in that spot.

The technician wiped the little bit of blood off his chin and sprayed him with a strong smelling mist. "Okay, here comes the new one. This shouldn't hurt at all going in, but the spot will sting for a while," she said, sounding bored. Dex didn't feel anything as she grabbed his lip with a different tool and he heard a sound like a wet towel tearing.

"Alright, we're all done," she said, wiping her hands on her dark blue uniform. Thanks for choosing Barrett and Brar."

Dex rolled his eyes and said, "Oh, please, not here, too."

The tech did a quick double take, then grinned. "Here too," she said. "Have a good time with that," she said, winking broadly.

"I'll try," Dex said.

CHAPTER THIRTY-TWO

BACK AT HIS apartment, Dex started to get the feeling back in his lower lip. It didn't hurt exactly, but it felt odd. He ate a food brick and that was fine, so he figured he'd better try out the new node. He was nervous — he had never wanted this upgrade and he was afraid of what it would be like. But he had done it now and rolling back would be an expense he didn't need. He knew he could just get a dampener if it was too much. But he needed to know what to expect before he met Annabelle in M City.

He linked in to Three Card Monte's, hoping that the familiar environment would make the experience easier. At first, everything seemed pretty much the same, but he knew that it wouldn't last. He walked, successfully over to one of the tables in the darker corner and sat. He managed the maneuver perfectly well, but it was profoundly disconcerting to feel the softness of the banquette's seat hit his ass, when he was already seated in his chair in the apartment.

It got weirder when he ordered a drink. The glass appeared on the table in front of him like usual, but when he went to pick it up he yelped. The glass was cold and wet. Dex tentatively reached out for the glass again and forced himself to hold on as he felt the cold, hard, damp container. It was just a glass. It felt just like a glass. But it wasn't real and Dex couldn't get past that. He kept going, though, and brought the glass up to his lips. He could feel its coolness before he touched it and he could smell the dark spicy sweetness of the rum and ginger beer he'd ordered. He took a sip and felt the cold, wetness of the glass on his lips, then cool liquid splash across his tongue. He swallowed and felt the drink go down his throat and into his stomach. It was utterly surreal.

He pulled up his pack of virtual cigarettes. He felt the box in his hands, so real he refocussed on his apartment to see if he was grabbing the table or something. But, his hands were still, sitting on the sides of the chair, holding nothing. He could still feel the small box in his left hand. He was starting to acclimatize to the strange sensations. It reminded him of the first visual displays — in fact it wasn't anywhere near as bad as learning to read a screen overlaid in front of real vision. But he had learned that trick more than thirty years before and even though he was nowhere near Malone's age, he still felt like an old dog.

He unfocussed and went back to his pack of cigarettes. He pulled one out and sniffed it. A tangy, toasted smell seemed to permeate his nostrils. He put it between his lips, feeling the spongy tightness of the filter. He lit it and drew in the smoke. He didn't taste much, since he still only had the basic node for translating virtual taste, but as he inhaled he could feel something in his lungs. It wasn't a burning sensation — it didn't feel like smoke at all, just a pleasant tingle. He blew out a plume of blue smoke and felt his lungs contract again.

He sat at his table in Monte's smoking his cigarette and finishing his drink. By the time he was down to the last few melting ice cubes in his glass, he felt like he could handle a basic experience without freaking out. He had learned to tune out the sensations in his physical body, of him sitting in his chair in his apartment and focus only on the feelings created by the combination of M City's simulators and his new node. He set his glass down on the table and stood. He walked out of Monte's and on to the street in Chandler's. It was raining, as usual, and the drops were cool on Dex's skin. He put on his hat and felt the circumference of the band tighten on his head. He walked, for maybe a half hour, just getting used to the feeling of his new virtual body.

When he logged out of M City and refocussed on his apartment, Dex found that his body was cramped and tired. He stood and stretched, then drew a large glass of water. As he drank, he thought that his experiment hadn't gone so badly. Tomorrow night with Annabelle, though, would be very different. He wondered if he'd made a terrible mistake.

As he was thinking dire thoughts, his system pinged. "Speak of the devil," he said when he answered.

"Talking about me?" Annabelle asked. "To whom? And what do you mean, devil?"

"It's just a figure of speech, kiddo," Dex said. "And I was actually just thinking about you, not talking about you."

"Well, that is what a girl likes to hear," Annabelle said. "I'm almost done with the list you gave me," she continued, "and there's still no hits. I've got about ten names left, so I hope we get lucky on one of those..." Her voice trailed off.

"I think that might be a dead end," Dex said, excitement in his voice. "But it's okay. I may have stumbled on to something, thanks to my good buddy Pat Malone." Dex explained Malone's guess about the killer being an employee of Gractor Devices and his own investigation of their existing and upcoming products. "I bet I've got the list of their local employees in my messages now," Dex said, "Let me just check." He logged in to the Cubicle Men's system and copies the list over to Annabelle's mailbox. "I've sent it over to you."

"I think we should just abort the current search," Annabelle said. "I can't do them concurrently and this Gractor thing seems like a way more likely lead."

"I agree," Dex said. "There are a lot of names on this list, more than the previous one. Is there any way to speed this process up? I don't know if we can afford another week, let alone two."

"The only way is to run the script from multiple sources," Annabelle said. "I've been using my own system, but I can run a clone out of the organization's box, too. I might be able to pull in a few favours for a few cycles elsewhere — I'll see what I can do."

"I know you will," Dex said. "So, we're still on for tomorrow?"

"You betcha," Annabelle said. "I've got a surprise for you," she added, in a coy voice.

"You do, now," Dex said. "Well isn't it just a small world. I've got a surprise for you, too."

"Ooh," Annabelle said, "battling surprises. How exciting. So we'll meet at Monte's then see where things take us?"

"Exactly," Dex said, nervous at the thought of what he was planning, doubly nervous at the thought of Annabelle's own surprise.

"Good," Annabelle said. "I'll get started on those scripts and I'll see you tomorrow." She ended the call and Dex drew a deep breath. What had he gotten himself into? Now that he'd said something to her, there was no way to pretend that nothing was up. He had no Plan B to fall back on. He got up and poured himself a drink. Nothing like a little liquid courage, he told himself. If only he could figure out how to drink in the real world while doing — never mind.

He went back online and started organizing things for the following night.

CHAPTER THIRTY-THREE

THERE WAS NOTHING new or different about the place — it was just Monte's, the same as it had always been. But to Dex, it felt as if it were unfamiliar territory. He dressed in his usual outfit: charcoal pinstripe suit, black shirt, matte wingtip brogues on his feet, battered felt fedora on his head. For amusement, nostalgia and maybe even some kind of lucky charm, he'd worn what he once thought of has his "date tie." It was bright crimson and when he'd put it on for his first date with Annabelle back when they'd been working the Velasquez case, he'd realized that he looked whorish at best and idiotic at worst. She seemed to like it fine, though, and ever since she'd always been happy when he wore it. It seemed appropriate this night.

He'd warmed himself up at the apartment with a pair of stiff shots of rum, since he wasn't about to add experimenting with stims to the night's festivities. He could feel the strange combination of his physical stomach warmly working on the Jamaica's Best and what he thought of as his virtual body sipping a stim-free dark and stormy. He found himself nervously playing with the pack of cigarettes on the table, flipping the pack over and over with the fingers of his left hand.

Annabelle materialized in the middle of the room, where Monte's link brought people in. She had dressed up, too; not quite as fancy as she had for their first date, but very nice nonetheless.

She wore slim gold trousers with a gauzy cream coloured top that Dex swore was transparent when he wasn't looking right at her, but that he clearly could not see through when his eyes were on her. It was a great effect.

She walked up to the table and came around to the side where Dex was sitting. She leaned toward him and Dex could smell some kind of spicy perfume. He'd never noticed that before, though he didn't think the new node had adjusted anything in his sense of smell. Dex closed his eyes and felt wisps of Annabelle's hair on his face as she leaned in and kissed him on the cheek. He didn't even know how to describe that sensation. It definitely did not feel like the times she had kissed him in the physical world, but it wasn't exactly bad. He was going to be okay, he thought. He could do this.

"Are you okay?" Annabelle said, a puzzled look on her face and Dex wondered what it was that had given him away.

"Sure," he said, smiling. "It's just, you know, a little weird."

"Yeah," Annabelle said, sighing. "You'd think that by now we'd be past all this juvenile drama, but things do seem a little odd between us, I admit."

"It was a pretty odd weekend," Dex said, smiling.

"That it was," Annabelle agreed. "But I've hatched a plan to make things better. Maybe."

"Oh," Dex said, raising an eyebrow.

"Yes," Annabelle said. "Look in your messages." Dex frowned and paged over to his inbox. There were two copies of notifications, one of a reservation for the following weekend at The Red Fish Inn and one for a transatlantic flight.

"You're coming back?" Dex asked, bewildered.

"Yeah," Annabelle said. "I figured that the next physical world meeting is going to be even worse than this, so we should just get it over with. Besides, we didn't actually talk all that much last weekend." She grinned and Dex blushed. "I really do think we're making progress, it's just gotten all weird all of a sudden. The only way to fix that is to spend time together and it can't all be here."

Dex was stunned. He wouldn't have been surprised if Annabelle had refused to visit him again, refused to let him see her in Nice. This was totally out of the blue. He didn't know what to say.

"Is this a problem?" Annabelle asked. "I thought you'd be happy," she said, confused.

"It's not," Dex said, "I am. This is great and strange and..." He didn't know how to express himself, so he leaned across the table and took Annabelle's hands in his. He squeezed and then just held them lightly. "I have something for you, too," Dex said, as he absently stroked Annabelle's hand with his thumb.

She looked at her hands, then looked back at him. "Something's different," she said. "You've done something, haven't you?"

Dex smiled. "Check your inbox," he said. He waited a moment, then saw the look on Annabelle's face change from one of confusion to surprise.

"I don't know what to say," she exclaimed. "I don't know what baffles me more — that you've booked us a room in a hotel or that you booked us a room in that hotel. That place is so expensive, I don't know anyone who's ever even stayed there."

"Well, nothing's too good for my girl," Dex said, hoping his nervousness wasn't showing through.

"But, you didn't answer my question," Annabelle said. "You've done something to yourself, haven't you?"

"Just catching up on the upgrade treadmill," Dex said, grinning.

Annabelle stared at him. "Are you sure about this?" she asked, her voice serious now. "You don't have to do this, just because of what happened last weekend."

"That's not why I'm doing it," Dex said. "I'm doing it for a lot of reasons, but the only one that matters is that I'm doing it because I want to be with you. Here, out there, it doesn't matter.

What matters is that we're together." He looked in her eyes and thought he saw them shining a little more than usual.

"You big softie," she said. "Well, let's not waste all that cash you're spending, shall we?"

"Indeed not," Dex said, standing. "Let's blow this joint." He took her arm and said, "Wanna walk?"

"I'd love to," she answered and they walked out the door of Monte's and into the light rain of Chandler's.

• • •

The walk to the Imperial Palace was not long, but they took their time. They walked arm in arm down the dark street and Dex got used to the heat of Annabelle's body pressed next to him. By the time they got to the opulent front portico of the hotel, they were soaked by the rain. As soon as they stepped under the roof of the entranceway, they dried off. It was an odd sensation, Dex thought, to be cool and wet one second and warm and dry the next.

A bot doorman held open the heavy looking crystal door of the building and Dex stepped back to let Annabelle go through first. He heard her gasp as he followed behind her. The place was impressive — the first thing you noticed walking in was the waterfall in the middle of the atrium. Looking up, you couldn't see where it came from and the sound seemed to thunder around them. Around the cataract were jungle foliage, flowers, birds and other creatures from the ancient world or some designer's imagination; Dex didn't know. It was like stepping onto another planet.

Dex followed a path laid out for him over his vision to the concierge and checked them in. The desk attendant handed him a small glowing jewel, apparently the room key. "Would you like a direct link to the room, or would you prefer to take the scenic route?" the bot asked.

"We'll walk," Annabelle said. "Can I get directions?"

"Of course, madam," the bot said and smiled.

"Got 'em," Annabelle said to Dex and took his hand. "Let's go." They walked around the jungle, toward a spiral ramp inlaid with gold. They walked up the helix, which wound behind the waterfall and through the trees and vines. After ascending for about a half minute, they stepped off on another level of the building.

"The room's this way," Annabelle said, squeezing Dex's hand. They walked down the hall, which seemed to be made of ice, embedded with precious jewels. There was a glow which came from behind the walls, bathing the area in a cool light. They came to an ornately carved door and Annabelle touched the glowing jewel to the jamb. She stopped and looked up at Dex. "Last chance," she said. "If you want to escape, now is the time."

He looked down at her, seeing the nervousness, hope and desire in her eyes. "I'm not going anywhere, kiddo," he said, leaning down and kissing her full on the mouth. He felt sensation explode in his lips, soon radiating through his body. It was not exactly sexy, but it wasn't all bad, either.

He didn't know how it happened, but all of a sudden they were in the room, the door closed, falling over each other and on to the giant pile of cushions which took up most of the space of the room in lieu of a bed. As he felt Annabelle slide her hands inside his suit coat, Dex had the incongruous thought that it didn't feel like her, like maybe he was with some other woman. He looked at her avatar, recognizing her smile. For a moment it seemed like this was all going better than planned.

He watched as she deftly removed his jacket and threw it on the floor next to the cushions. He felt his heart race as her fingers worked the edges of his shirt; tiny feathers on his skin. Who designed these sensations, he wondered. How was this exact feeling programmed? His mind was all over the place and when he felt Annabelle's lips on his bare chest, he had to force himself not to pull away. He let her kiss him, then when she tilted her head up to breathe, he slipped his hands under her blouse. She wore nothing underneath and Dex marvelled at how much it almost felt like warm human flesh under his fingers. He tried to put the strangeness of the sensation out of his mind, as he carefully watched Annabelle's reaction to his touch.

Her eyes were closed and when his hands found her breasts, they fluttered for an instant. Dex smiled and for the first time that night felt something real in the pit of his belly. When his thumb grazed her nipple, Annabelle made a soft noise halfway between a moan and a gasp. And Dex stopped being able to think about anything after that.

CHAPTER THIRTY-FOUR

THE MAN WAS angry. The candidate was no longer in the city. It turned out that she had only been visiting when he'd chosen her and now she was halfway around the world. In Europa, of all places. She might as well be on the moon.

He had never failed to work with a candidate before. Even that horrible woman who thrashed and fought, who he'd had to beat with his fists to keep quiet, even she had been successful in the end. This was not acceptable.

It had been a bad day. He was scouring the 'nets for information about his candidate in the morning before work when he'd stumbled over her real location. He had spent the workday fuming after he had learned that Annabelle Lewis, his candidate, his choice, was gone.

As he was walking into his apartment, he was still looking at the proof of his failure. "How can this be?" he'd exploded. Gerry, home early, was just coming out of the lav.

"Whoa," Gerry said, stepping back. "Are you okay, man?"

The man hadn't expected his roommate and now confronted with his presence, his rage found a target. He moved quickly to the surprised man and let his momentum carry them both into the still slightly damp lav. Gerry was much larger, but surprise and hate made up a strong advantage. The man looped his right foot around Gerry's ankle and jerked. The two of them went down, the man falling hard on Gerry's ribs. He heard the bigger man let out a small grunt of pain, which fuelled him on even more.

He grabbed Gerry's head and bashed it against the solid floor of the lav. He hit the man two, three, four more times, until the back of his head was pulpy. He thought he could even see a few of the small silicon implants coming out in the goo. As soon as he saw the blood, the rage abated and soon left him. He stood, stripped off his clothes and washed himself. The autoclave would get the blood off his clothes, as it always did. He would have to deal with Gerry later. Now, he needed stims. Lots and lots of stims.

• • •

The next morning, when he got to his workstation, he found that he had a new product for testing and was expected to start right away. He stormed into the manager's cubicle and slammed his hand on the small desk.

"This is bullshit!" he'd screamed. "How am I supposed to test these things?" He threw the tiny wrist mounted stunner on the desk. "No one gave me specs, no one gave me the calibrations scripts. This is bullshit," he repeated.

The manager, a giant of a woman the man knew only as Hayes, barked out his name in a dismissive tone. She thumbed the door close button and the wall behind the man closed off as she stood behind her small desk and towered over the small man. "Calm down. The specs and calibration scripts are on the bulletin board. There's no need for this kind of behaviour. What is wrong with you?"

Her stern tone ripped the man out of his rage and filled him with shame. "I'm sorry," he stammered. "I've been under a lot of stress and it just seemed..." he struggled for an excuse. "I don't want to get in trouble," he finally said in a small voice, his eyes locked on the floor.

"You're a good employee," Hayes said, "but past performance doesn't excuse this kind of stunt. This is going on your record with a warning. This is your only free pass. Anything, no matter how trivial, after this and you're out on your ass. Understood?"

"Yes, sir," the man said, looking at his feet.

"Now I want you back at your station and get started on these tests. We have a large order from an important client and need these shipped as soon as possible." Hayes sat back down and dismissed him with a look.

He went back to his station and downloaded the specs and scripts he needed. As he started updating his equipment, he began to feel angry again. Hayes had made him feel small, made him feel insignificant. He knew that he wasn't small or insignificant, though. Gerry knew, too. He was powerful, with important work. He would show them.

CHAPTER THIRTY-FIVE

DEX DIDN'T EXACTLY feel like a whore. It was much more pleasant than that. He had had a surprisingly good time with Annabelle, though he was tired now. Dex had hired the room for six hours and they had determined to get the most out of it. Now, the morning after, he sat at his station at B&B, doing his job as well and with as much enthusiasm as an automaton would, but his mind was on the events of the previous night.

He figured that he had been fairly unimpressive as a lover. He'd never done anything like that online before and moving around in M City isn't quite as simple as just thinking about it like the ads say it is. He'd fumbled his way through, helped along by Annabelle's guiding touch and more enjoyable audio cues, but it was definitely not stellar. After, she had seemed so happy, though, that Dex couldn't help but feel proud. And that made him feel quite strange now.

He knew that Annabelle was no stranger to a man's avatar and his new node got a workout in that room in the Imperial Palace. He had to be honest with himself, it had felt good. But when it was over and they lay in each other's arms, the feel of her head on his chest felt just wrong enough to make him remember that he was really in his apartment, wearing the ugly one piece, alone.

It was a difficult feeling, knowing that she had enjoyed herself so much more than he had. As he looked up a user manual for a disk upgrade node, he wondered if that was how she felt after last weekend. He wondered if it was the kind of thing you could ask your lover. "So, it was great for me, but how horrible was it for you?" Though it hadn't been horrible. It had just been fake.

• • •

Over the next few days, Dex and Annabelle spoke every day. It was less awkward between them than it had been after Malone's retirement party, but they both knew that their relationship had changed dramatically. They spent most of their time talking about the case. Annabelle had found a handful of other systems to run her scripts and they were cranking away at a much faster pace. Even so, she projected that it would take several days before she got through the whole employee list.

"I've set a notification for you on all of them," she said. "In case I'm busy or something when a match comes through, both of us will get the ping. I also set up an automated search string to run when I get notified of a match. We'll have a full dossier on any matches within a half hour."

"Great work," Dex said. "Can you copy me on the full bios, too?"

"Already done," Annabelle said. "Anything I get, you'll get."

"I just hope it comes through in time," Dex said.

"Me, too," Annabelle said. There was a silence between them, both of them thinking about the victims and their mutilated bodies.

"What do you think the stims are all about?" Annabelle asked eventually. "Why do you think the killer hits them with the neurostims?"

"I've thought about that," Dex said. "I first assumed it was just to keep them all compliant, but a stunner would do that just as well. I wonder if the killer likes to pretend that they want it, that they are asking for it. I'd guess that with enough neurochems swimming around in my system, even I could be persuaded to be into having my skin flayed off."

"Jesus, Dex," Annabelle said.

"Sorry," he said, chagrined. "But you know what I mean. If our killer is sufficiently nutso, which seems like an eminent possibility, I wouldn't find it too odd to discover that the crazy fuck thinks that it's all a consensual act."

"What is wrong with people?" Annabelle asked.

"I don't know what makes some people do terrible things," Dex said. "Not like this. I've got no sympathy for these kinds of people at all."

"It must just be a problem with brain chemistry," Annabelle said. "I bet with the right drugs, this killer could become normal again."

"And what does that accomplish?" Dex asked, bitterly. "It won't bring back Luis Harker or Hazel Ramer. It won't change anything that happened for them. And what about those people and the people who cared about them? Nothing is going to make them normal again."

"That doesn't mean we shouldn't try to help someone who is sick," Annabelle said.

"I think that's exactly what it means," Dex said. "Someone does something like this, it's game over. No a second chances." Neither of them spoke for a moment.

"Well, we just disagree," Annabelle said, with finality.

"I guess that's okay," Dex said. "If we were totally compatible it would be boring." Annabelle burst out laughing.

"Oh, Dex," she said. "Sometimes I don't remember why I stay with you. And then there go, being your annoying, difficult, utterly wonderful self and I can't imagine life without you. Don't ever change."

"Too late, kiddo," Dex said. "Or have you already forgotten our wild night about town." He put on a silly voice to cover up for his nervousness. He hadn't meant to bring it up, but he couldn't take it back now.

"Aw, honey," Annabelle said. "You haven't changed a bit. Gizmos and gadgets don't make you who you are. You just operate more universally now, that's all." Dex laughed and Annabelle joined him. They were safe for another day.

They kept on chatting for another few minutes then Dex noticed Annabelle pause in mid-sentence. "What's up?" he asked.

"Have your checked your messages recently?" Annabelle asked, her voice tight.

"No," Dex said, his heartbeat increasing. "Why? Has your script turned up something already?"

"No," she said. "It's a message from Zizou. We all got it. Pat Malone died this morning."

CHAPTER THIRTY-SIX

THEY DIDN'T WANT to be alone, so they went to Monte's. No one had organized anything, but they found half the squad already there when they arrived. Annabelle got a round for the table, setting Dex's no-stim dark and stormy in front of him. On a private channel, she said, "You might want to fix a real one."

"I'm already ahead of you, kiddo," he answered.

The table was full of the usual crowd, with the addition of the captain. When everyone had gotten drinks and made the usual noises, she called for attention. "This wasn't exactly a surprise," she started. "We all knew that Pat didn't have much time left, but I for one had hoped that it would be longer than it was." There were murmurings of agreement around the table. "Pat was the street lieutenant when I took on the captaincy and he was more of a help that I ever let you all know. I think it's safe to say that Pat taught me more about this squad than I ever could have learned on my own. He was a fabulous leader, a great member of the team and a wonderful man. I will miss him, more than I want to think about now." She lifted her glass high and in a voice marred by only a slight tremor, said, "Here's to Pat Malone."

"To Pat Malone," a chorus of voices answered her and everyone took long pulls on their drinks. The talk amongst them turned to their memories of Pat. Jay Shiraishi, one of the longtime goon squad members held court, having worked with Pat the longest.

"There was the one time," Jay said, "we were on this incredibly boring patrol. There had been some muggings on Upland Drive, so we'd been showing the flag, you know, just being present. Nothing had happened in over a week, so there was absolutely nothing to do. There weren't even any bars or cafés in the place — just boring residential blocks and minimarts. I was going snake by the second hour of the shift and I think I was probably annoying the hell out of Malone." A few of the folks who had worked with Shiraishi laughed knowingly.

"So, he decides that we need to do something to make the night a little more bearable, you know? And so he says to me, "Okay, kid, here's the thing. For the rest of the night, no touching the ground. Your feet touch the ground, you owe me a beer. And not a pisswater minimart special or a virtual brew, either. The real thing, home-brewed by a master. You make it and I swing it so you never have to walk this beat again. Deal?' I'd been stuck on watchman duty for months, so of course I took the bet. And for the whole rest of the patrol, I was jumping from front steps to fence posts, climbing signs and generally making a monkey out of myself. I swear, I never heard a man laugh like Malone did when I finally was done that shift."

There were more stories and more drinks and after a while Dex found himself alone at a table with Annabelle. He was on his fourth or fifth drink back at his apartment and he'd lost count of the number of refills Annabelle had had. He never knew what she was really consuming anyway, so counting never did much good. "I'm going to miss him," Annabelle said.

"Me, too," Dex said. "I never really got to know him until recently, but he was one of the good ones, you know? I really liked the time I got to spend with him. It's just a shame it took so long." He paused and took a long pull on his drink. "You know, it's funny, I never really socialized with anyone on the squad — well, with anyone at all really, not for a long long time. But these last few months," he let out a long breath. "Shit, it takes me back, you know?"

"No, I don't," Annabelle said, kindly. "You never really talk about your past. It's like it's this dark shadow looming behind you. We all know it's there, but it's so insubstantial that there's nothing anyone can do about it."

"We all have things hiding in our pasts, Annabelle," Dex said. "Even you."

"Sure," Annabelle said. "I think you know most of my secrets, though."

"Maybe," Dex said, "maybe not. It doesn't matter." He shook a cigarette out of the pack and lit it. They sat silently for a while, Annabelle watching Dex and Dex staring at nothing.

"So, who was he?" Annabelle said, eventually.

"Who was who?"

"The one who got away."

"What makes you think that's what it was?"

"I pay attention to you, Andersson Dexter," Annabelle said, smiling. "And there are the things you say and the things you don't and there's all the stuff in between. So who was he? You played music together, right? And then he left you and broke your heart."

"What do you know about it?" Dex said, raising his voice and glaring at Annabelle.

"Nothing," she said, softly, reaching over and taking Dex's free hand. "That's why I'm asking."

Dex sighed, the anger leaving him. "His name was Maks. Maksym. And it's not what you think — we were just friends. Well, it wasn't 'just' anything, but we weren't lovers. I don't know if things would have been any different if we had been. I used to think so, but now..."

His voice faded and Annabelle waited while Dex remembered. After a while she said, "So what happened?"

"He grew up," Dex said, his voice resigned. "And I didn't. Or at least not right then."

"And that's when you stopped playing music," Annabelle said.

Dex nodded. "That and a lot of other things, too."

"You know," Annabelle said, squeezing Dex's hand, "someone once told me that people change. It's what we do. You're not the same man who lost Maks, but you are who you are partly because of him. He's still in your life, just like you're still in his, just like Pat Malone is still in ours. You never really lose anyone, Dex. They're just hiding."

Dex looked at Annabelle. "Sometimes, I don't know what I did to deserve you," he said, smiling at her in the half light of the bar.

"Same to you, buster," she said. "Same to you."

CHAPTER THIRTY-SEVEN

THE DAY AFTER the impromptu wake for Malone, Dex woke with a raging hangover and an unshakable feeling of urgency to find the cutter. He even checked his messages as soon as he was upright in case he'd missed a notification while he was passed out, but there was nothing. For the next two days, every time his system pinged, he jumped, thinking it was Annabelle's script notifying him of a match. Every time it was something else, he was filled with a sense of foreboding and worry that they still were not on the right track. And in between these worries about trying to stop the killer, Dex did some serious thinking about his life.

He thought he had figured out a plan which was, if not fool-proof, at least something which solved some of the obvious problems in his current existence. He spent his evenings researching his options and eventually came to a decision. It would take some doing, but Dex had figured out a way to get free from the crushing treadmill of crappy jobs. And he thought it might have the pleasant side effect of making things easier with Annabelle. Maybe.

Dex was at work at B&B when Annabelle's flight arrived. Dex didn't know where she found the extra days off, but he wasn't about to complain. They would meet at Annabelle's hotel after he was done for the day — neutral ground. It wasn't even lunch time and Dex was already nervous.

• • •

The nervousness only got worse. By the time he was on the train back to his apartment, he was a mess. He showered and changed and as he dressed he could barely close his suit, his hands were shaking so hard. His eyes strayed up to the cabinet with the bottle of rum, but his stomach rebelled at even the thought of a drink. He was on his own.

The walk to The Red Fish Inn felt somehow both infinitely long and instantaneous. Dex paused before walking through the hotel's big steel door and took a deep breath. Come on, man, he chided himself silently. It's only Annabelle. She likes you, remember? He sighed and walked in to the lobby.

He bypassed the check in kiosk, with its small ID chip reader/ writer and started looking around for Annabelle. He found her sitting on the small settee in the lobby. She stood when she saw him and came toward him. She stepped into his arms and they embraced lightly. "Wow," Dex said. "What is happening to us?"

"Evolution?" Annabelle said, as she broke away. "I don't know. But I think it's a good thing. It mostly feels like a good thing." She took Dex's hand and they both sat on the small couch.

"When are you leaving?" Dex asked.

"Day after tomorrow," Annabelle said. "First thing in the morning."

"So we have all day tomorrow, then," Dex said.

"Yes and two nights," Annabelle said, looking away.

"Right," Dex said, squeezing her hand involuntarily. "Well, we can cross that bridge when we come to it."

"Which will be in a few hours," Annabelle said.

"But we have a few hours to put off that conversation," Dex said. "What do you want to do until then?"

Annabelle thought for a moment. "How busy do you think that place where Pat's party was would be about now?"

"I doubt it will be empty," Dex said. "But it won't be like last weekend."

"Why don't we try that?" Annabelle said.

"Are you sure?" Dex said. "We could just hang out here, or at my place or..."

"No," Annabelle said. "I want to go out, do something normal. We don't have to stay long if it gets weird."

"Okay," Dex said. "Let's go."

• • •

The Cog and Sprocket was fairly quiet that early and they found themselves a table near the door on their own. Dex ordered a pint of the fine dark ale and Annabelle stuck with the bubbly water. "How's this?" Dex asked when their drinks arrived.

Annabelle took a sip. "Actually, this is pretty nice," she said. "It's almost like being in Monte's."

Dex laughed. "It is, isn't it," he said. They sat together in companionable silence, watching the other people in the bar and sipping their drinks. Finally, Dex broke the silence.

"So," he started, "I've been doing a lot of thinking lately."

"Are we going to have another big state of the relationship talk already?" Annabelle asked.

"Actually, no," Dex said. "This is something else." He took a pull on the beer. "I know you've suffered through me complaining about my job many times."

"Many, many times," Annabelle agreed.

"And I've told you a few times about how I didn't always live this way, like a regular working stiff."

"Back when you were a musician," Annabelle said. Dex just nodded and Annabelle just waited for him to continue.

"I feel like a large part of who I am is trapped in my past," Dex said, eventually. "I have this strange feeling like I want to lose myself in my memories of that time, but there's a lot of pain back there, too."

"I'd be happy to hear you talk about it," Annabelle said, her eyes full of concern.

"I know," Dex said. "Maybe one day. But that's not what I want to talk about now. No, I just mentioned it because for a long, long time I've felt like my life isn't the one I'm supposed to be living. You know what I mean?"

"Dex," Annabelle said, reaching out for his hand. "You know I do."

"Of course," he said, flushing. "Obviously, you understand. Anyway, I've been doing a lot of figuring and research and I think I've made a decision. It's a big decision, so I wanted to talk to you about it before I did anything I couldn't get out of. But I need you to know that I think my mind is made up." Dex looked at Annabelle and he was sure he could see her heartbeat as she worried about what he would say next.

"I'm going to quit my job," he said, finally.

Annabelle just stared at him for a moment, then burst out laughing. "That's all?" she said. "After all this preamble, I was sure you were going to say something, I don't know, a lot more shocking than that."

"I don't just mean I'm going to get another job," Dex said. "I'm quitting the whole thing, this whole stupid life that I hate. I ran the numbers and I make enough to keep myself afloat from the cases alone and I have enough savings to get myself into one of those new freelancer housing cooperatives in Europa." He paused and took Annabelle's hand. "I've already put in an application and it's been provisionally accepted. I'm moving to Nice."

• • •

Annabelle was stunned. "You're what?" was all she managed to get out.

"There are three completed freelancer housing complexes in Europa — one in Edinburgh, one in St. Petersburg and one in Nice.

Since one of the problems I had was that with the severely reduced income, I wouldn't have enough spare cash for trips to see you, it seemed obvious to just pick the one in Nice. Things wouldn't really have to change much; I bet I could even get the same deal that you have and stay on the same squad. And you wouldn't have to travel so far either." Dex looked at Annabelle's shocked expression. "I thought you'd be happy," he said, confused.

"It's just so... so sudden," Annabelle said. "I wasn't expecting anything like this. I mean, we've been doing well, but I don't think we're at this stage yet. I mean, it wasn't too long ago that we were both terrified of even talking to each other. Hell, Dex, don't you think you're moving a little fast here?" Annabelle had sat back in her chair, even moved it away from the table a little bit.

"I don't understand," Dex said. "I mean, this doesn't have anything to do with us, not really."

"Moving to Nice doesn't have anything to do with us?" Annabelle countered archly. "Moving half way around the world, to the town where I live, every day, every night, doesn't have anything to do with us? Come on. You can't really believe that."

"I'm not trying to move in with you," Dex said, his voice rising now. "Things wouldn't have to change at all, except for the flights. I mean, you came all this way to see me just now, with all the hassle and expense. When I live there, it would just be a short train ride at most. But I'm not expecting that we'd be hanging out every day or anything. I don't understand why you're so upset."

"No, you don't," Annabelle said and stood. "And I can't seem to explain it to you, so I'm leaving."

"What?" Dex said, shocked.

"I'm just going back to the hotel," Annabelle said. "I need a little time to think things over — I'm not leaving town. I'll see you tomorrow," she said.

Dex stood. "Let me walk with you—"

"No," Annabelle said. "I said I need time and that's what I mean. I'll be fine; I'm not some delicate flower who needs protecting. Just leave me alone for a while, okay." She was almost pleading, so Dex just sat back down, dejected. "We'll talk tomorrow," Annabelle said, as she walked to the door. "I promise."

CHAPTER THIRTY-EIGHT

ANNABELLE WAS ANGRY with herself. She wished she hadn't walked out on Dex, but she just couldn't stay in that place anymore. She needed time — time to deal with his decision, time to deal with her own feelings. She knew Dex didn't understand why his plan to move to Nice bothered her so much, because she never wanted to tell him that the very fact of the distance between them was one of the things that helped her continue on in their relationship. She could always get away, she could always go home. With him living in the same city, there would be no escape.

Annabelle got off the train and started walking the few blocks to the hotel. She knew she had overreacted and there was nothing for it but to talk it out with Dex. He'd been honest with her after last weekend and she knew it wasn't easy for him. It was her turn now. She just wasn't ready for it yet.

She was lost in thought and focussed on the map overlaid on her vision as she turned the corner to the street with her hotel. She didn't hear the shushing sound of the electric motor, the scooter stopping behind her or the footsteps of the scooter's rider. So when, all of a sudden, she felt someone's presence behind her, it startled her out of her thoughts and brought her focus fully and completely on her physical self.

She turned toward that feeling of another body much too close to hers and without even thinking about it, she brought her right arm up, the fist balled. She felt it connect with something soft before she even saw the man. She heard an oomph sound and felt a hand lock on to her arm. Automatically, she twisted away and out of the corner of her eye she saw a flash of something metallic near her face. She felt a crackle of electricity and jerked her head away. The hand was still a vice grip on her arm.

"You came back," she heard a voice hiss out of the darkness. "You came back for me. Why are you fighting?"

The voice snapped her out of fight or flight and she paused, trying to make sense of the words. She could see the man close to her, his face nearer to hers than she could stand. She was scared — there was no doubt in her mind that this man meant her harm. But driving her more than her fear was her disgust at his closeness, the sheer heat and smell of him, so she mindlessly tried to pull away from him. He tightened his grip on her arm and started dragging her toward the scooter. She could see an expandable case on the back of the scooter and knew that the man was trying to pull her toward it.

He was still trying to get her with his stunner, or whatever it was, so she was twisting to keep her face as far from him as possible, but it was keeping her off balance and making it easy for him pull her toward the box. The lid of the box was hanging open, the interior like a dark cavern she knew he was trying to get her into. She also knew that if she went into that box, she would never make it through the night alive.

In what felt like a thunderbolt, she suddenly remembered training from what seemed like a million years before, when she was in the army. Once she had left the service, she always thought of that time with regret, as years wasted on a future she never even really wanted. Now, though, she thanked all those men and women who had beat into her a sense of physical survival.

She let the man pull her again toward the box, trying to act as if she were tiring from the game of tug of war. When she saw his attention wander off her for a moment, she stepped in toward him, letting his own strength propel her toward him. As they got closer, she threw out her left arm to block his hand and its metallic stunner. She knew she only had one shot at this, or he would get her with the device for certain. With all her weight and momentum behind her, she dealt him a vicious head butt, connecting her forehead with the bridge of his nose.

He yelped, dropping the stunner as he brought his right hand up to his ruined nose. Her blow hadn't knocked him out like she'd hoped, but had loosened his hold on her arm. She twisted out of his grip and aimed a swift kick at his midsection. He dropped and she turned and ran without stopping to see what happened to him.

• • •

She was in her hotel room, sitting on the floor with her back to the locked and bolted door before she fully understood what had happened. Her hands were shaking and her heart pounded in her ears. She felt like being sick, like laughing, like crying until her body ran out of tears. Instead, she just sat on the floor, staring at the small bed with its silver sequinned cover, hugging her knees tightly to her chest.

She didn't know how long she had been sitting there when she finally recognized the soft noise in her ear. Her system was pinging her, had been pinging her relentlessly for a better part of an hour. She blinked a few times and realized that her eyes were wet, that she had been crying without even knowing it. She wiped her eyes and focussed on her display. It was Dex calling. He had been calling for most of the night.

She answered, finally, and when she heard his voice say, "Annabelle, finally. I'm so sorry..." she burst into tears again.

"I don't really understand," he said, "but obviously this isn't going to work. I'll move to St. Petersburg; I'll find a way. Maybe I'll get a part time job, I just don't want—"

"I think I met the cutter tonight," Annabelle interrupted him, her voice stronger than she imagined it could be after her ordeal. "He tried to put me in his box, but I got away. I got away," she repeated as her voice broke. "I got away."

"Oh my god," Dex said. "Where are you? Are you okay? I'll be right there. Wait, do you need to be alone? Do you need a doctor?" His questions came in no particular order; he realized he was babbling.

"I'm okay," Annabelle said. "I'm not cut; he didn't get me with the stunner." She sniffled and got a hold of herself. "Dex, I'm at the hotel. Please come. I need you here with me."

"I'm on my way."

CHAPTER THIRTY-NINE

THE MAN LAY on the ground, doubled over. The pain in his nose was sharper, but the pain in his gut was what consumed him. He heaved, but nothing came up. It felt like an eternity before he was able to get himself to his knees and even longer before he could stand.

He limped to the scooter, blood still pouring from his nose, staining the front of his shirt. He thumbed the scooter to life, then pointed it in the direction of his apartment. He needed to get cleaned up, needed to get control back. How could this have happened? She had come back, come back for him. Why else would she have come back to the city, if not for the work. If not for him?

He hadn't even planned on doing the work tonight. He had intended to do something with Gerry, who was still occupying the lav in the apartment. But when he had brought the scooter up to load Gerry into the trailer box, his system notification had gone off. He'd forgotten that before he'd discovered that Annabelle Lewis actually lived in Europa and wasn't just going to be gone for a few days, he'd tagged his system to notify him when she returned to the city. After he'd learned that she was probably never coming back, he'd forgotten all about it.

But then the ping sounded and everything changed. She was back. He was in control after all, his choice would be honoured. He left Gerry and taking only the tools he needed, he'd straddled the scooter and headed out into the night.

He'd found the dark corner near her hotel and waited. She had taken her time, but he followed her signal from the pub where she and that man had gone. His heart was racing as he watched her close on to his location and was nearly vibrating with excitement when he first saw her. He stepped toward her, newly tuned Joybuzzer in his hand ready to make her ready, when he felt her fist connect with his midsection.

None of them had ever fought before, not at this stage. And why would she fight, this one who was lost to him then miraculously returned? He had made his choice, the end was inevitable. She must have known, or else why would she come back to him. Why?

• • •

He made it back to the apartment, plugged the scooter into the floor socket to recharge and managed a shower even with Gerry blocking most of the space in the lav. He crawled to his bed and passed out.

Chapter Forty

When Dex got to the hotel room, Annabelle was in pajamas, curled in a ball under the covers on the bed. He had been talking to her the whole time he walked from his apartment to the hotel, but he still had to confirm that it really was him at the door before she would disengage the locks and remove the chair she'd wedged under the knob. When she opened the door and saw him there, she collapsed into his arms.

"Did you get him?" she whispered as she clung to him.

"There was no one there," Dex said. "It looked like there was some blood or something at the corner, in the doorway of the supplement shop."

"I guess that means I didn't kill him," Annabelle said, sniffling and starting to pull away from Dex. They walked back into the hotel room awkwardly, Annabelle refusing to allow Dex to let go of her completely. Dex shut the door behind him and he heard the thunk of the lock as Annabelle's system re-engaged the deadbolt.

"Guess not, kiddo," Dex said, walking her back to the bed and sitting beside her. He pulled the cover over her, wrapping it around her shoulders. She had been shaking since he'd arrived and she was still shivering, though the temperature in the room was higher than normal. "You want to talk about it?" he asked, gently.

Annabelle shook her head. "I just want to forget it," she said, wiping her nose. "I've never been so scared. All I could see was that box clamped behind that scooter. He was going to put me in it, I know he was. I can't stop thinking about it. I close my eyes and there it is — dark and small. It was the most terrifying thing I've ever seen." She buried her face into Dex's shoulder and he just held her. "I wish I could just forget it all," she whimpered.

They sat that way for a long time. Finally, Dex said, "I know you want to forget it, but our memories make us who we are. Even the hard ones. Maybe those ones the most." He stroked her hair and sighed deeply. "You're a strong person, Annabelle," he said. "Stronger than anyone I know. This won't kill you, not even close. You've been through so much more than this — I know you can handle it. If anyone can, it's you, kiddo." She didn't answer, just held on to Dex as if he were the only thing keeping her from falling off an apartment block rooftop.

• • •

Eventually, Annabelle pulled away and padded into the lav. Dex heard water running and rushed to the door. "Wait," he shouted. "You'll have evidence on you..."

Annabelle opened the door and stood just on the other side of the threshold. She smiled, but her eyes were vacant. "I already took the swabs," she said. "Blood on my hand, my sleeve where he grabbed me. The physical specimens are over there," she pointed at the table, where Dex saw a piece of fabric and a sample cloth each in their own silvered sterile bags. "I did it while we were talking; the scans are already being analyzed."

"Jesus, Annabelle," Dex said. "I can't believe you managed to do all that."

"It was your voice," she said, softly. "As long as I could hear your voice, I knew there were things I had to do. I didn't have to think about — about what happened."

"Oh, kiddo," Dex said, his voice cracking. He took a step toward her, but she raised her hand.

"Don't you fall apart on me, now," she said, tears coming to her eyes. "I can't handle that. Just let me wash my face and then we'll see what we need to do, okay?"

"Okay," Dex said, fighting for control. When Annabelle closed the door, Dex wiped his eyes and fought down the tears that were threatening to take over. He couldn't believe how strong she was. Not only had she fought off a killer who had taken at least six other people, but she'd had the presence of mind to send her own samples in. It would have been better if she'd waited for him, but he couldn't fault her that. He knew that if it had been him, he'd have been in the shower long before he even thought about evidence.

He logged into the case file and saw that Annabelle had, indeed, scanned and logged the two samples and that the system was extracting DNA and other evidence from them now. She had even set the system to search for a match among all the male employees on the list from Gractor.

"You did all this while I was coming over?" he asked aloud as Annabelle returned from the lav.

"I did the online work while I was in the shower," Annabelle said, sitting in the chair by the table. "I didn't want to feel anything, you know, here," she said, her voice quiet. "It's always easier for me if I'm online."

"I know," Dex said, sitting on the edge of the bed. He looked at her and wondered at how the fragile woman before him, who couldn't even look at him, could be the same person who did everything else she had done that night.

As if reading his mind, Annabelle said, "It's like it was happening to someone else, you know? Like I was just watching it all from a metre away. When I got back here I think I just shut off for a while; I don't remember doing anything until we talked. Then it was like it was someone else again — I just had tasks to do, things to accomplish. If I just plug away at the work I don't have to think about anything. But now..." she looked at Dex, then quickly looked down again. "Now, it's there, in the back of my mind and I can't make it stop."

She started to cry, very softly. Dex didn't know what to do, whether he should get up and go to her or leave her alone. He just sat on the bed, watching. "Oh, Dex," she said between her tears, "those poor people." She lost it then, weeping openly. Dex went to her and kneeled in front of her, his arms around her. She leaned into him, sobbing into his shoulder.

"It's okay," he whispered. "You're safe now; I'm here. And we'll catch this bastard, you and me together. He won't hurt anyone else, I promise."

Dex stayed with Annabelle for the rest of the night. He put her to bed, promising to stay in the chair, which did. He didn't think he slept at all, instead he watched Annabelle as she tossed and turned fitfully, even though he'd made her take a draught of SleepingJuice. When she woke early the next morning, he kept his distance but made sure she knew he was there. He was too tired to be surprised when she asked him to join her in the bed.

He climbed in next to her, the previous night's clothes still on and put his left arm over her. He burrowed his face in her hair and held her tightly. "Don't leave me," he thought he heard her say, but he had closed his eyes and sleep was descending on him, so it might have just been a dream.

CHAPTER FORTY-ONE

WHEN THE MAN came to, twelve hours had gone by. He gingerly got up and stepped over Gerry's body to look at his reflection. His stomach hurt and his nose looked pretty bad, but he wouldn't be stopped in the street. Especially not where he was going. Plenty of folks down in green sector looked worse than he did.

He changed clothes and put his tools back into his pockets — 'buzzer in the right pocket, knife in the left. He liked the feel of passing the knife from hand to hand between cuts. He fingered the hilt of the weapon as he unplugged the scooter, the smoothness of the worn bone calming him with every stroke. Annabelle Lewis had gotten away for now. But the night was full of possibilities, of other choices to be made.

He parked the scooter in a small alley near the stim bar and walked around to the front door. The place was dark, as they usually were, the bartender a tall, blonde woman who looked like she wouldn't put up with any bullshit in her place. That was fine; the man didn't intend to do anything inside the premises.

He ordered a Peach Soda, a mild sedative with clarity overtones and waited as the woman mixed the cartridge. He waved his hand over the till, paying for the cocktail with an anonymous cash transfer via the chip in his hand. He took the cartridge over to a small table and shot half the load while he scanned the crowd.

He hadn't been in a place like this in several months, but it was the usual scene — most of the folks lost in their private worlds, some so far gone they were gaping and drooling on themselves. A few chatting amiably and there was always the couple or group who were obviously only minutes away from one of those charge by the hour rooms down the street. The man ignored them.

He focussed on the loners, the ones who were staring blissfully at nothing, or half smiling to themselves at some private thought. He finally decided on the tall, thin man at the bar. Happy, but not out of his mind. Exactly the right kind of person for a potential candidate.

He didn't believe in fate, but he knew he had made a good choice when the thin man got up to leave just as he'd downed the last of his Peach Soda. He turned in the empty to the recycler by the bar and followed the man out the door a few steps behind. His luck continued, as the man turned into the alley where he had parked the scooter. It wouldn't be like Annabelle Lewis would have been, the man thought to himself in a moment of self-pity, but as soon as the 'buzzer was in his hands all his thoughts turned to this new candidate.

He slipped in behind the man, cleared his throat and when the man turned, he shot his arm forward. This time, the 'buzzer connected solidly with one of the man's many facial nodes and he went down in a heap. In no time the man had his candidate safely in the box and was on his way to brown sector.

CHAPTER FORTY-TWO

DEX WOKE WITH a start. At first he didn't know where he was or why he was there, but then the night's events slowly came back to him, like the memory of a nightmare. He rolled over carefully, to find the rest of the bed empty. He reached over to the rumpled sheets where Annabelle had lain. Still warm. He sat up and looked around the small room.

Annabelle was at the small cupboard area, heating something in the zapper. She hadn't heard Dex stir and he watched her hunched shoulders as she waited for the machine to finish. He didn't want to startle her, so made sure he made some noise as he got out of the bed. At the sound of his rustling, she turned and smiled.

"Morning," she said. "I've got some coffee going, it should be ready in a few minutes."

"How are you feeling?" Dex asked, watching her with concern.

"My arm hurts," she said, lifting the sleeve of her top to reveal a livid purple bruise on her upper arm. "Otherwise, I'm just dandy." She smiled ironically and turned back to the zapper as it beeped. She opened the lid and took out two large mugs of steaming coffee. "Pale and sweet, right?" she confirmed, handing Dex the cup.

"Just like me," he answered, grinning. He didn't know if this forced domesticity was the right thing for either of them now, but what else was there to do? Annabelle was obviously fine physically and Dex was the last person to know what to do for whatever trouble her mind was in.

"Just like you," Annabelle said, her eyes twinkling again for the first time since before she had left The Cog and Sprocket. Dex marvelled at what a good night's sleep could accomplish.

He sat at the small table and sipped at the coffee. Annabelle made a great cup; so much better than the swill at B&B... "Oh, fuck," Dex muttered, looking down at the coffee cup.

"What?" Annabelle said, her tough veneer cracking as her voice trembled slightly.

"Oh, nothing, really," Dex said, "I just realized that I'm supposed to be at work right now and I'm pretty sure I'm all out of second chances. I guess I'll be quitting a little sooner than I had planned." He smiled, hoping that they weren't about to get into another argument.

"Why put off until tomorrow what has already been done by mistake today?" Annabelle said. She looked at Dex and her smile faded. "And in that seize the moment vein, I'm really sorry for the way I reacted last night at the bar."

"No," Dex said, "It's not your fault. I shouldn't have sprung it all on you like that..."

"Maybe not," Annabelle interrupted, "but I still overreacted. I know you're not trying to change anything between us with this move, it was all just me." She looked away, cradling her coffee cup in her two hands. "I've always just thought of the distance between us as an escape valve, you know? Like a natural barrier that we could use — no, that I could use when things got too tough. Even with everything that's happened between us lately, all the changes, I never thought that that distance would disappear. And I didn't realize how much I was clinging to it until you said you wanted to move to Nice."

She turned back to face him. "I'm sorry, Dex," she said. "I didn't want you to know how much I needed that space, that easy way to get away."

"It's okay, kiddo," Dex said. "I know you need your independence and with so much happening between us we both need to be able to have time away from each other. If the Barcelona complex was done, I would have picked that one, but the other two just seemed too far. Though, it would still be closer than we are now, so we could manage, I guess. I don't think I could afford to visit as often as I do now, but..."

"No," Annabelle said. "I doesn't really matter, I see that now. I thought having an ocean between us made a difference, but the real distance between us is the same whether we are on opposite sides of the world or opposite sides of the same bed." She came over to the table and sat on its edge next to Dex. "If it's what you want, move to Nice," she said. "Or move to St. Petersburg. I'm pretty sure I can afford that train ride and I've always wanted to see the North. But whatever you choose, do it because that's what you want, not because I got hysterical in a bar."

Dex laid a hand on Annabelle's knee and was sure that she didn't flinch at all. He looked up at her and felt something brewing in his chest. He'd felt it before, but tamped it down. It was old and familiar and while it felt good it also gave him a dreadful feeling that things couldn't possibly end well. "Aw, kiddo," he said, but his next words were stilled by an insistent ping from his system.

He saw in Annabelle's eyes that her system was going off, too, and they both knew that this meant only one thing. They had finally gotten a match from the Gractor employee list. They both went online and in seconds Dex was updating the case files with the new information and sending all the data on this match to every squad member in the city. Annabelle was searching for as much information on the suspect as she could get while downloading images, addresses and maps to their systems for instant access. The

name they both would remember without help — Harold Arturo
Bolick.

CHAPTER FORTY-THREE

THE SQUAD CAPTAIN, Zahara Zhang, called Dex as soon as she got the case update. "You make sure you take at least a pair of Shiraishi's folks with you before you hit the apartment. I don't need to tell you that this guy is armed and dangerous and after getting the shit kicked out of him last night is probably more than a little pissed off. Speaking of which, how is Lewis holding up?"

"She's a champ," Dex said. "But you want to ask her yourself, she's right here with me."

"I'll call her next," Zizou said. "You be careful, Dex."

"Always, cap," he answered with more confidence than he felt. He had arranged with Jay Shiraishi, Malone's replacement as the new lieutenant of the street team, to meet with two of his goons at a small café around the corner from Bolick's building. He and Annabelle were on their way to the rendezvous point, Dex coordinating with the goon squad and Annabelle setting up a real time tracker on Bolick. With some highly illegal maneuvering, Annabelle would be able to see where Bolick was, in the physical world, using the feed from his onboard system. They would be able to find him wherever he was, however the process was far from instantaneous. Annabelle wasn't even sure how long it would take to get it going; she'd never done it before.

The information they already had showed that Bolick had entered his apartment late the previous night. According to the building's logs he hadn't locked the door from the outside since. Without the tracker up and running, it was all they had to go on.

Annabelle and Dex stepped into the small coffee shop and Dex's overlay pointed out his contacts at a small table near the bar. The two women, Julianne "Jules" Rudolf and Dot Kuhns were each sipping from tall to go cups and drumming their fingers on the table. Dex noticed Kuhns checking the time compulsively. Jules stood as Dex and Annabelle approached the table and walked up to Annabelle, her hand extended.

"Nice work," she said, shaking Annabelle's hand. "I heard you were never on street, but you've obviously got the chops." She nodded pertly at her partner, who also stood.

"Let's go get this motherfucker," Dot said, her right hand straying to the knuckledusters on her belt.

Dex turned to Annabelle. "You don't have to come up with us," he said. "You can stay here if you want."

"Don't patronize her," Jules said. "She kicked that fucker's ass once already, I think she deserves to see him go down."

"It's okay," Annabelle said to Rudolf. "This has been really hard for me and not just for the obvious reasons. He isn't being a dick, trust me." The short, fireplug of a woman grunted, but backed down. Annabelle turned to Dex. "That being said, I do want to see this piece of shit taken down. I'm coming with you."

Dex nodded. "Okay," he said. "Let's go."

• • •

There was no response to their knocking at the door, so Dot used a chip scanner banned in every jurisdiction Dex could think of to bypass the door's simple ID chip-based security. It shushed open after she activated the small handheld device and the two goons entered the apartment. They each took one side of the door, weapons drawn.

"Harold Bolick," Jules said, in a loud clear voice. "Show yourself." Nothing happened. Dex and Annabelle were waiting in the hallway for Jules or Dot to give the okay for them to enter the apartment. It seemed like an hour had passed before Dot appeared at the door, a dour look on her face. "He's not here," she said. "But he was."

Dex followed Kuhns to the lav, where the body of a man was lying in a pool of blood. His head was a bloody pulp and Dex turned away. Annabelle was on her way to the lav to see what the commotion was and Dex walked into her still moving body, forcing her away from the gruesome sight. "You don't need to see that," he said, as she peered over his shoulder.

She caught just a glimpse of the mess on the floor and said, "Jesus, is that him?"

"No," Jules said, emerging from the lav. "I'm guessing it's the roommate, but we won't know for sure until the scans are in."

"How do you know it's not Bolick?" Dex asked.

"Too tall."

Annabelle slumped down to the floor, her eyes unfocussed.

"You okay?" Dex asked, sitting down next to her.

"I'm looking for him" she said, her eyes dancing back and forth as if reading something only she could see. "I've got him tracked to a five kilometre radius, but that's just not enough." Frustration filled her voice.

"Send me the map," Dex said, a dark idea spreading in his mind. Almost as soon as he finished the sentence, his system pinged and a map of the city appeared on his display. The image centred on circle which showed the area Bolick was currently in. The circle encompassed a hodgepodge of neighbourhoods, but Dex felt his blood chill when he saw what he'd feared — one of those neighbourhoods was brown sector. Where Bolick had taken all his victims.

• • •

Dex and Annabelle left Rudolf and Kuhns to take care of the

mess in the apartment and caught a train to brown sector. En route, Dex called Jay Shiraishi and filled the new lieutenant in on what had happened.

"You'd better get a move on," Shiraishi said. "I got a message from Melissa Vonruden about ten minutes ago. She recognized the image you sent around of the perp. Seems that she ran into him at her day job."

"What does she do?" Dex asked.

"She tends bar at a stim joint in green sector," Shiraishi said. "And she's certain your man was in, not even an hour ago."

"She's sure?" Dex asked, his heart racing.

"Yeah," Shiraishi said. "She said he looked like he'd gone one round too many with a mean drunk, but it's him. And he left following another guy out."

"Oh shit," Dex said. "Jay, we need everyone you've got in brown sector to search the abandoned buildings. He's got another victim, right now."

"I've only got two pair on the street," the lieutenant said. "I'll get them working the grid right away, but don't you have anything more than just someplace in brown? Anything to narrow it down a little?"

Dex looked over at Annabelle, who was still working away online. "Not yet, but soon, I hope."

"Well, let's just hope it's soon enough," Shiraishi said.

• • •

Dex and Annabelle got off the train in the middle of brown sector. Shiraishi had patched Dex in to his teams on the street, so they could match their search to the grid Shiraishi had laid. As they approached the first building, Dex turned to Annabelle. "I want to tell you that you don't have to go in there," he said, "but I can't. It's just you and me for now. If anything happens Shiraishi's people will be here within minutes, but we're on our own up front. Do you think you can handle it?"

Annabelle focussed back on Dex and managed a smile. "It doesn't matter what I think," she said. "What choice do I have? I can't let something awful happen just because I'm a little shy."

Dex put his hand to her cheek. "You're incredible," he said.

"And don't you forget it, mister," she said. "Okay, let's get it over with."

CHAPTER FORTY-FOUR

THE FIRST BUILDING was empty, but they didn't know that until they'd searched every room. They stayed close together, trying to be as quiet as possible, but Dex was sure that anyone could hear the tattoo their racing hearts made and the rasp of their shallow breaths. When they finally got out of the dilapidated old warehouse, both of them were drenched with sweat.

"I have to tell you," Annabelle said, when they were on their way to the next location, "this really is a pretty terrible date." Dex laughed, all the way down to his belly and Annabelle joined in. They stood on the street, the two of them looking like they hadn't seen the inside of a lav in days, laughing their heads off.

Finally, they stopped and Dex looked at Annabelle. "When this is over," he began, but she put a finger on his lips.

"Later will take care of itself," she said. "Let's just get this done, okay?" Dex nodded and they walked the three blocks to the next building on their list.

They had crawled into a small opening which Annabelle was sure would emerge in a large room, when both their systems began an insistent chirping. They stopped and each of them answered the call. "I've got it," Annabelle whispered.

"Me, too," Dex said, as he saw a map of brown sector appear before his eyes. A small green dot appeared at one corner, the dot representing Harold Arturo Bolick. He was in a building only two blocks away and he wasn't moving.

"Back up," Dex said, urgently, starting to crawl backwards into Annabelle.

"I'm going as fast as I can," she said, as she backed out of the small tunnel.

"I've notified Shiraishi and the street team to meet us there," Dex said. "We're the closest, so we'll probably get there first."

"Fine," Annabelle said, "if we ever get out of this goddamned hole." Dex could hear her voice getting higher and her breath was coming faster and faster.

"It's okay, kiddo," he said, trying to calm her, "we're almost out now. Just a few more metres." He could hear her ragged breaths, but she kept moving and soon she was out of the tunnel and heading for the door of the building. Dex followed quickly and they were on the street, running toward the green dot.

As they ran, Dex pulled a stunner from his pocket. "Take this," he said, pressing the small object into Annabelle's hand. "Just in case."

"You need it," she said, her breath heavy.

"I've got other stuff," Dex said, pulling a set of tarnished knuckledusters and a sedative spray from his pocket. "I'll be okay." Annabelle nodded and pocketed the stunner. They turned a corner and slowed, approaching the building where Bolick was waiting.

"We can't wait for the goons to catch up," Dex said quietly as they walked to the broken door of the decrepit old one storey building.

"I know," Annabelle said, a steely look in her eye. "I'll be fine. Let's go get him."

• • •

They sidestepped through the doorway, slipping beside the door on its broken track. The map showed that Bolick was in a room just to the east of their position, through a hallway and around a corner. Dex opened an audio channel between himself, Annabelle and the rest of the team. "We're in the building," he sub-vocalized and looked at Annabelle. "I'll go first, you follow and cover me." She nodded and crept behind Dex as he crabwalked down the small hallway.

There were boxes and bags all over the floor, the place covered with the detritus that streeters leave when they've decided a place is too destroyed even for one of their squats. One of the outside walls had a ragged hole through it and some previous resident had tried to patch it with what looked like an amalgam of old food wrappers and glue. Mixed in with the other trash were patches of broken tech, bundles of unbearably filthy clothes and some kind of sticky goo that Dex refused to contemplate. He ignored it all, but moved carefully so as not to disturb the mess and give themselves away.

As they reached the corner, they could hear voices. One voice was low and they couldn't make out the words, but the other one seemed to be laughing maniacally. Annabelle made to move in, but Dex put a hand up. "Two voices is a good sign," he said. "Let's not blow it now." He crouched and moved silently around the corner, edging to the other side of the wall. Annabelle crept around the corner, staying on the inside. There was a closed door just in front of them.

"Shiraishi," Dex said and he and Annabelle heard the lieutenant reply. "What's the ETA on the cavalry?"

"About a three minutes," he said.

Dex looked at Annabelle, who shook her head. "Not fast enough," he said. "We're going in."

"You don't have to do that," Shiraishi said.

"Damn it," Annabelle broke in. "He's got someone in there with him. Did you even look at the images of those bodies, you fucking—"

Dex cut her off. "We're going in, Jay. Get your people here as soon as you can."

"Roger," Shiraishi said.

Dex turned to Annabelle and gestured to the door. "I'll knock it down, then you go in and take the left. I'll take the right. Just stun anyone you see and we'll sort it out later. Got it?"

"Got it."

Dex stood and aimed a hard kick at the spot next to the door-knob. The door cracked and half of it fell into the room. Annabelle was through the small gap before Dex had time to think and as he pushed the remains of the door aside, he heard the sound of a stunner go off. As he entered the small room, he smelled a raw, human stink before he saw the man tied to a chair, slumping forward, two long cuts on his naked torso.

Dex heard an electrical pop, like a stunner going off, and the man in the chair fell forward, limp. He took a step forward, then heard a voice to his left say, amazed, "You came back," and simultaneously the sound of a stunner clicking ineffectually in rapid succession. Before he could even turn toward her, Dex yelled, "Thumb the reset!" at Annabelle. He turned and saw Bolick and Annabelle, the man with his arms around Annabelle's neck.

Dex began stepping forward and pulling his arm back, knuckle-dusters already covering his fist with their crackling electricity, when he heard a sickening crack. He saw a body slump toward the floor and a combination of terror, rage and indescribable sadness momentarily paralyzed him. "Annabelle," he choked out, then heard the clatter of a steel-bladed knife falling to the grimy floor. His eyes followed the knife up to the hand which had just before been hold-ing it and he realized that he'd gotten it backwards.

Annabelle was holding the lifeless body of Harold Bolick, a look of cold rage on her face. Her right hand was still on his left cheek, his head at an impossible angle to the rest of his body. She looked at Dex and when their eyes met she finally dropped Bolick. He slid to the floor like a sack of vatmeat. Annabelle let her hands drop to her side and let Dex come toward her and put his arms around her. "It's over," he said, stroking her hair. "It's over, now."

She pulled away and blinked the tears away. "I stunned him," she gestured at the inert and bleeding man in the chair without looking at him. "But he needs help — he's cut pretty bad."

Dex left her and went to the man on the chair. He was alive, but bleeding a lot from the cuts on his chest. Dex was undoing the bindings which held him to the chair when the four members of the goon squad burst in.

"Where's the perp?" a tall, broad shouldered man demanded.

"Dead," Annabelle said, pointing at the body on the floor.

"This guy needs help," Dex said, pulling the man out of the chair and into the arms of two of Shiraishi's people.

"Consider it done, sir," a familiar voice said and Dex recognized Eduardo Lino. "I'm glad to be here for this and I can't say I'm too sad to see it end this way." He gestured at the body on the floor. Dex shot a look at Annabelle, but her expression was unreadable.

"Just take care of this guy," Dex said and walked back to Annabelle. He took her hand in his and after a beat she slowly looked at him.

"Let's get out of here," he said. She nodded and they walked out of the building.

Chapter Forty-Five

IT HAD BEEN a couple of months since Annabelle had killed Harry Bolick and a month since Dex arrived in Nice. Dex was working a case about a stolen objet d'art for one of his neighbours in the housing cooperative and slowly building a reputation in Nice. He had managed to stay on at the squad, but Zizou suggested he might want to make nice with the local captain at least. Dex had met the man a few times for cocktails at a local café — Le Rétro was no Cog and Sprocket and René Biagini was no Pat Malone, but Dex liked the local beer and the local captain's company well enough.

After the regular meeting with Zizou's squad, Dex found himself still in Monte's after the usual crowd had left. It was only him and Annabelle and she had been tying one on a little more than usual. Thanks to Biagini, Dex had found an excellent liquor store locally and he'd been treating himself to a couple of rounds of rum and water. They were both a little looser than usual and Annabelle suggested a change of venue.

"Let's walk," she said and Dex agreed. He took her arm and they walked into the dark, rainy streets of Chandlers. "How's your new place?" she asked, as they walked under the weak yellow light of a streetlight.

"I'm getting used to it," Dex said. "I still bash into the table in the middle of the night when I get up to take a piss, but otherwise it's fine." Annabelle laughed. Dex's new apartment was smaller than his old one, but it was noticeably nicer. It was a modern multiuse design, so the table and two chairs concealed the main cupboard, zapper and recyclatron. He actually had more usable room, even though the place was a good 10 square metres smaller than his old apartment.

Of course, Dex's place couldn't hold a candle to Annabelle's apartment, but with the pay cut he'd taken by giving up his job at B&B, he was lucky to have gotten as nice a place as he did. And he rarely had the opportunity to be envious; he was now only a quick fifteen minute train ride away from Annabelle's place, but he'd only been over there once since he moved. He had promised not to push things once he arrived in Nice and he hadn't. He could wait. He could wait a lifetime if he had to.

"Actually, it's a great place," he continued. "I haven't managed to ruin it with all my junk yet."

"What junk?" Annabelle asked. "Now that you don't have a work uniform any more, you hardly have any stuff at all."

"There's my mandolin," Dex said, a wounded look on his avatar's face.

"Which you wouldn't even have if I hadn't given it to you," Annabelle said. "For someone who likes the physical world, you don't show it, mister."

"There's more to the world than stuff," Dex said, smiling. "I'd love to have you over sometime," he continued, "I could play for you..." He felt her stiffen against his arm. "I'm sorry," he said, quickly. "I'm not trying to pressure you into anything, I was just talking."

"I know," Annabelle said. "It's just that after everything that happened, I just feel a little..." Her voice trailed off. "Fragile, I guess."

She hadn't ever talked about what happened in that small room in brown sector and every time Dex had tried to bring it up she either changed the subject or just left. He'd stopped trying. Now, he cautiously said, "I know how things can haunt a person."

"This isn't just any old thing," Annabelle stopped and turned to face Dex. "For christ's sake, I killed a man. With my bare hands; I broke his neck."

"You had no choice," he said.

"There's always a choice, Dex," Annabelle said. "And we know which one I made." She turned and walked a few steps into the darkness. "I was only just getting used to it," she said, in a small voice.

"Used to what?" Dex asked, confused.

"This," Annabelle said, her hands pointing at herself. "This body of mine. I was almost feeling like it was part of me, part of who I am, who I want to be. Then it went and..." She choked back a sob. "I never wanted to do anything like that, not even to someone like him. Not ever." Her shoulders shook and Dex knew she was crying. He walked up behind her and carefully put his arms around her.

"He would have killed you," Dex said, turning her to face him. "When he got you on the street, he was going to cut you just like he cut the others. And he wouldn't have stopped with you. He wasn't going to ever stop, Annabelle, you have to know that."

"I don't know," she said, her eyes welling up again. "Maybe I should just have let him..."

"Don't ever say that," Dex said, sharply.

"What?" Annabelle said. "I'm useless, now. I'm worse than I ever was — I can barely leave my apartment, Dex, I'm so scared of being touched. I can hardly even concentrate on my job; I haven't picked up a case since it happened. Hell, even in here in M City I'm no good any more." She looked away from him and said quietly, "I know you're only still with me out of pity..."

"That's the dumbest thing I've heard in a long time," Dex said.

"Sure, I wish things were different, who doesn't? But we get what get. And what do I have? I have a beautiful girlfriend, who is smart, strong and the toughest person I've ever met. Don't you fall apart on me now."

Annabelle looked up at Dex. "You really think I'm strong enough for this?"

"Hell yes," Dex said. "You'll get through this, I know you will. It just takes time. And I'm a pretty patient guy. Besides, if you never come see my apartment, I never have to tidy it up." He grinned.

Annabelle smiled, weakly. "I'm glad you haven't lost your sense of humour."

"You haven't either," Dex said. "It's just hiding. But I mean it, Annabelle. If you can never be with me out there again, I can live with it."

"Are you sure?" Annabelle asked.

"Yes, I'm sure," Dex said and took a breath. "I love you, Annabelle Lewis and whether I'm with you in here or out there, that doesn't change it. I'm here for you. Wherever you want me, however you'll have me, I'm yours." He reached out to touch her face and she walked into his arms. She lifted her face and they kissed, holding each other in the darkness of the virtual street.

ACKNOWLEDGMENTS

This book was begun on passage from Costa Rica to Ecuador, and finished at Puerto Amistad in Bahía de Caráquez, Ecuador. I was definitely influenced by the experiences I had and the characters I met along the way, particularly the kids from *Kamaya* and *Victoria* (Maya, Kai, Thomas and Patrick). See, I really was writing a book after all.

Also, thanks to all my many supporters around the world: you have no idea how much I appreciate all your notes of encouragement and your patience with my slow responses. Special thanks to Steve Southwood on *Dignity* for catching those embarrassing typos, and to Richard and Krista on *Lilith* for being our mail drop.

And of course, thanks to Steven: my editor, first mate and best co-conspirator. In that way you are the Annabelle to my Dex.

ABOUT THE AUTHOR

M. Darusha Wehm is a two-time Parsec Award finalist and author of the SF novels **Beautiful Red**, **Self Made**, **Act of Will** and **The Beauty of Our Weapons**.

Her short fiction has appeared in *Thaumatrope* Magazine, Podioracket's *Glimpses* anthology and *Luna Station Quarterly*.

In the physical world, she was a civil servant with the Government of Canada and is now engaged more or less full-time in writing.

She is based in Victoria, BC, Canada and is currently living in New Zealand after sailing down the west coast of the Americas and across the Pacific Ocean with her partner, Steven, on their sailboat, Scream.

For more information about her writing and her travels, visit Darusha on the web at http://darusha.ca.